Krist

HOLIDAY TERMINAL

GWYN MCNAMEE

CHRISTY ANDERSON

GWYN MCNAMEE
&
CHRISTY ANDERSON

♡- Gwyn McNamee

XO-Christy Anderson

Holiday Terminal

© 2019 Gwyn McNamee & Christy Anderson

Two people who are meant to be together will always find their way back. They may take a few detours, but they are never lost.

This book is for all those following a detour...

ACKNOWLEDGMENTS

We have had such an amazing time co-writing this story. Thank you to all the beta readers and all those who have helped share their love of *Holiday Terminal*. We cannot express how much we appreciate your support.

CHAPTER 1

PENELOPE

"M a'am. I'm sorry, but the storm is just too dangerous for us to continue. I'm gonna have to land." The voice of the pilot crackles over the headset, giving me the worst news possible.

Crap.

Snow falls so thick outside the tiny airplane window, it's practically a whiteout. It only confirms what he just said. I'm screwed.

This is what I get for trying to fly home on Christmas Eve.

I glance over at Max and Mom, both fast asleep in two of the other seats on the small plane. They're not going to be happy about missing Christmas with Dad, but it's not like we have any choice. God or Karma or whatever power is out there, obviously doesn't want me home for the holiday.

It's just a crappy end to an already crappy day.

The landscape below us is almost invisible, completely blocked by the raging storm.

Where are we, anyway?

I press the button on the side of the headset I'm wearing so I can speak with the pilot. "Okay. Where are we setting down?"

"The nearest airport is Millerton Field. A small strip in Tennessee near the North Carolina border."

Wonderful.

I sigh and drop my head back against the plush leather seat. Everything went downhill almost the moment I walked into that meeting today. Aaron was running late, which delayed the start. Then the prospective client got a phone call he had to take during the meeting, which meant we didn't get out of there until three hours later than planned. Now...this.

Why can't I catch a break?

I really need to see Dad. Sometimes, the only thing that can cure what ails you is a big hug from the man who has given you unconditional love since the day you were born.

But maybe the storm will lift, and we'll be able to get out in a few hours. I need to keep my hopes up somehow.

We begin our descent. The snow thins slightly the closer we get to the ground. Though, I still can't see much. Hopefully, the pilot can.

Wouldn't it be just my luck to crash on Christmas Eve at some tiny airport in the middle of nowhere?

The plane connects with the tarmac, jolting us up with three bumps. Mom and Max both jerk awake and blink rapidly, looking around in confusion. I pull off my headset and hang it on the hook in front of me.

Mom's eyes meet mine. "What's going on?"

"We had to land. The snow is too heavy. It's too dangerous to stay in the air."

She glances out the window on her side. "Where are we?"

"Millerton Field, somewhere in Tennessee near the border."

"Oh, dear. Your father is not going to be happy about us not making it back tonight."

I sigh and rummage through my purse for my phone as we taxi down the runway toward a terminal I'm sure is nothing more than a one-room shack. "I know."

"We're not gonna see Grandpa?" Max's question, in that tiny, quivering voice, just about breaks my heart.

I ruffle his thick, dark hair and shake my head. "Sorry, kiddo. Doesn't look like it."

His wide blue eyes stare up at me. "But...how will Santa know where to bring my presents if we're not at Grandma and Grandpa's house?"

Oh no.

Presents.

I already sent everything ahead of us: gifts from me and the ones coming from "Santa," too. After everything he's been through in the last couple of months, Max deserves them all, and then some. This new job is taking more time and energy than I ever thought possible. I never imagined I would need to spend so many hours away from him, but if I have any hopes of working my way up, I need to do a good job. The best. Being hired on at this young age as a producer's assistant is practically unheard of. I can't do anything to prove Aaron was wrong in putting his trust in me.

The plane stops, and the engines wind down. Max gazes out the window at the winter wonderland. He doesn't often see snow in Nashville. Other than the big ice storm last year and our annual visits to North Carolina at Christmas, he probably would never experience anything truly winter.

The pilot emerges from the cockpit and offers a kind smile. "I'll take you in, and we can figure out what's going on with the storm."

"Are we going to be able to get out of here tonight?"

One of his shoulders rises and falls. His bourbon eyes

dart over to Max and soften. "I don't know. It isn't looking good."

Great.

I huff out a sigh and turn to Max. "Gather your stuff, buddy. Mom, help me get him out of here."

The dress and four-inch stilettos I wore to the meeting are probably the worst possible thing to fly in, let alone to wear while traipsing across a snow-covered and slick tarmac into a tiny airport building. But I didn't even have time to change before racing to the airport. We knew there may be some inclement weather, and were hoping to avoid it, but the meeting ran late, and the storm is much bigger than anyone anticipated.

It was the perfect storm to ruin my holiday and the first real break I've had since starting this job.

The pilot grabs the lever on the door and pushes it open, dropping the steps down and out into the snow. A gust of icy air swirls into the plane, raising goose bumps on my bare arms. Max shivers next to me, and Mom wraps her arm around him.

The terminal doesn't look any bigger than most gas stations.

Jesus. We really are in the middle of nowhere.

Mom helps Max out the door and down the staircase, and I follow on shaky heels. Bitter cold wind whips around us, and snow bites at my exposed skin.

Dang, that's cold.

I've never been a fan of winter weather, and after this experience, I may do even more to avoid it in the future. Maybe try to move to Hawaii...

The pilot grabs my hand to assist me down the last few steps, and I hustle as fast as I can without falling on my ass and grab onto Mom's shoulder for balance. Someone, who must be an employee of this place, tugs open the terminal door for us, and we step into the welcome warmth of the airport. If you can even call it that.

That's being generous. The building is really nothing more than one large, open room, almost like a hangar, with what appears to be a few small offices off to one side and bathrooms on the other.

If this is where we are spending Christmas, I am the worst mom in the world. I glance over at Max in Mom's arms and blink away the burn of tears forming in my eyes.

Don't lose it in front of him.

Our friendly pilot stands to our left, talking with the gentleman in jeans and a sweater who opened the door. Maybe he has some more information about this storm.

I approach them and plaster a smile I definitely don't feel onto my face. "Excuse me, but do you have an update?"

The employee frowns. "Sorry, ma'am. Things are looking bad for the next twelve to twenty-four hours."

Our entire Christmas...gone.

What a mess.

"If we're going to be stuck here tonight, is it possible to get our bags?"

The pilot offers an apologetic smile. "I'll make sure we get them off the plane, ma'am, just in case."

"Thank you, I appreciate it."

We're just going to have to make do with what we have. And it's not much. A quick second scan of the building reveals a few vending machines in the corner, old plastic chairs scattered around in seating areas, and a wall of windows that show nothing but white outside.

Wow. Merry Christmas.

ARTEMIS

I press the radio call button on the yolk. "Millerton Field UNICOM, Cessna N17771. Nine, zero, zero feet. Short final. Landing runway 02 full stop."

"Cessna N17771, Millerton UNICOM. PIREP zero five minutes ago reported visibility zero point five miles, winds one five at seven, gusting two five. No VFR. Do you have the runway in sight?"

An almost blinding wall of snow fills the windshield, and the yolk vibrates in my hands, battling against the gusting winds determined to take me down.

This is not how I want to spend my Christmas Eve.

I press the call button again. "Millerton Field, UNICOM, Cessna N17771, negative. I am on glideslope and sporadically see the field lights. I am landing."

"Cessna N17771, roger that. Report once on the ground and clear of the active."

"Millerton Field, will do."

I should already be in New York getting ready to attend the Warren holiday party, to schmooze with all the family's clients and plaster on a fake smile to make Mom and Grandmother happy for a while.

Actually, maybe this won't be so bad.

Except, I had other plans tonight. Big ones. Ones I wanted to take care of once and for all. Things that could only be done at the party in a very public manner.

I guess it'll have to wait unless the storm lifts and I can get out of here. Maybe I'll get lucky.

But that's unlikely. Luck hasn't exactly been on my side lately. It's been one shitshow after another, and today is just the culmination of a crap week. The meeting went as well as it could have, which means great things for the Warrens and not so great things for those poor fucks or my conscience, and now, this storm has ruined the one thing I've been looking forward to.

The snow driving against the windshield nears whiteout and makes the runway lights almost impossible to see. Time to get it down.

The wheels hit the tarmac, and I release the breath I've been holding the entire way down.

"Jesus, this really is the middle of nowhere."

Of all the places to hit trouble, why did it have to be here?

They rarely get snow here this time of year. This freak storm couldn't have come at a worst time or place.

"Millerton Field. Cleared the active. Where can I tie down?"

"Cessna N17771, take taxiway Bravo to the FBO at the end of runway 02. We have tie downs."

I direct the plane across the icy runway toward the small building that must be the FBO. One other plane sits already tied up.

Looks like I'm not the only poor asshole stuck here.

Getting out to tie down is going to be cold. The wind kicks up snow in the air, stinging my exposed face, and the icy slush soaks into my loafers. I grab the tie downs and attach them to the wings and tail. Then I snatch my briefcase from inside the plane and slip and slide my way into the terminal.

Finally...warmth.

I set down my briefcase onto the damp mat on the floor, then rub my likely frostbitten hands together.

Christ, it's cold.

We've gotten off easy with warmer temps lately in New York. And coming from Atlanta, I wasn't at all prepared for this. I didn't even bring a change of clothes since I had planned to head straight to the party as soon as I landed.

I also didn't expect to be in this tiny nowhere town. I am so dead when I finally make it home.

I kick the snow off my feet and take in my surroundings. The little terminal is nothing more than a modified hangar, but at least it's warm.

A small group of people stand together, talking near the offices. I shove a hand back through my wet hair, slicking away the snow and trying to regather some semblance of appropriate appearance.

"Remember, Artemis, you're always representing the Warren family anywhere you go. Do it well."

I grab my briefcase and make my way across the terminal toward the office and the men huddled together there. One looks like a pilot, who I'm guessing had to land here, and the others must be airport employees. They're no doubt discussing what they'll do if we are stuck here for the night.

God, please don't let that be a possibility.

It's been way too long and hard a road getting here, to the place where I'm ready to do what I planned tonight at the party. Putting it off isn't really an option.

I'm screwed.

I step up to the group and plaster on my best "Warren" smile. "I'm sorry to interrupt, any news on the storm? I really need to get to New York."

A tall guy with wind-swept, blond hair assesses me, his eyes scanning from the top of my head down my perfectly tailored suit to my loafers. Vastly different apparel from his jeans and sweater.

They probably don't get people like me here very often. And I can see why. This place is barely on the map.

But he offers me a friendly smile, nonetheless. "Looks like we'll be here a while. The storm system is spinning over us right now. We're keeping a close eye on it. We can let you know if conditions change."

Not what I want to hear.

But *"a Warren must present a proper and pleasant outward appearance at all times."*

So, instead of voicing my frustration, I plaster on a fake smile. "Thanks, that'd be great. My name is Artemis Warren. Please alert me of any updates."

I really don't need this tonight. Not on what was supposed to be the biggest night of my life up to this point.

At least where my career is concerned.

There were other nights, ones spent on a sandy beach with a certain brunette, ones I can't let myself remember. Because if I do, I'll dwell on what I've lost instead of keeping my eyes on my future, where they belong.

My shoes slip across the floor, and I grab my phone from my inside breast pocket while I head back down the short hallway to the doors I just came through that overlook the tarmac and this damn freak storm. It'd be beautiful if it weren't seriously fucking up my plans.

I scroll through my contacts, pull up the one number I least want to dial, and hit send.

It only takes two rings for him to answer. "Where the hell are you? I've been calling."

I roll my eyes at his gruff tone—one so familiar, it's almost the only voice I can hear in my head at times—then pinch the bridge of my nose. "Hello to you, too, Father."

A long, silent pause greets me. Then he sighs. "Sorry, Art. Just, tonight is a big deal. I need you here. Have you landed?"

He's going to love this. A tiny smile tugs at the corner of my lips. This change to his plans will piss him off. That makes me feel a little better.

I love the man, but we don't share the same vision for my life and the way it should be lived. I've let him control that for far too long.

Starting in Cape Harmony six years ago.

Even all this time later, I'm still letting this man get to me. I'm a damn adult. A successful attorney. A force to be reckoned with. But as soon as he opens his mouth or stares me down with those hard, icy eyes, it's like being that skinny, teenage boy all over again.

Visions of long summer days spent with a dark-haired girl who had freckles across her nose and sun-kissed cheeks flash through my mind. My lips curl into a smile, but I shake off the images.

I can't get bogged down in that.

Not again.

Those days are long gone. I was just a kid then. Young, dumb, stupid, and totally wrapped up in the "Warren" world.

I clear my throat and straighten my spine even though he can't see me. Force of habit. "Had to land in Millerton, Tennessee. A massive snowstorm reduced visibility to nothing. It's basically whiteout conditions here. I'm sort of stuck."

"Stuck? What do you mean you're stuck? When the hell can you leave?" His tone rises with each word.

My smile spreads even wider. "Father, I'm trapped here in this tiny airport until this shit-ton of snow stops falling and I can leave. I don't know when that will be. You may think you can control the world, but you can't control the weather."

His annoyed sigh grates on my nerves.

As if I'm the cause of this damn storm.

"The moment this storm dissipates, get your ass on that plane and get here. You're only a few hours away. The party should still be going if you can manage to get out of there soon. But you *will* be here, understand me, Art?"

Oh, I understand. Your precious plans are in jeopardy.

Well, so are mine.

I don't want to be stuck here, either. "I'll keep you updated, *sir*."

The emphasis I place on the final word was undoubtedly picked up by him and not appreciated, but I don't care anymore. He can be pissed all he wants. I push end on the call and shove my phone back into my pocket.

This is shaping up to be a Merry Christmas.

CHAPTER 2

PENELOPE

"**M**omma, I'm hungry."
Well, crap.

I glance around the tiny building they called a terminal and at the meager options available. A few vending machines with the usual snack items that are probably old and stale on the left wall near the bathrooms. This place can't get much traffic, and the people who do use it are probably local and aren't sitting around, munching on Fritos and granola bars after they land.

According to the pilot, this entire place was supposed to be shut down for the next two days. They hadn't planned on having any passengers or anyone needing any assistance.

The storm ruined everything.

"Let me see what I can find for you, buddy." I rub Max's back.

He nods and climbs up into Mom's lap.
Thank God, she's here.

If I had been alone with him, things would have ended up

even more messed up. We barely made it to the airport as it was with her packing him up and getting him ready. Thank God, Aaron offered me his plane. There's no way we would have made a scheduled commercial flight on time.

If I didn't love my job so much, I would be pissed about the meeting being scheduled on Christmas Eve. But I'm not in any position to complain to Aaron. He's the boss. He's the one who produces incredible music for multi-million-dollar recording artists. I'm just the lowly assistant, trying to claw my way up the ladder to become a producer myself one day.

And it will happen, or so Aaron promises.

All I need to do is keep busting my ass, and agreeing to things like meetings on Christmas Eve, to show how dedicated I am to learning the ropes and becoming as incredible as he is. Moving to Nashville with Max was a massive risk. Leaving behind Mom and Dad, my only support system, was gut-wrenching, but in order to establish a real *career* for myself, to build a real *life* for Max and me, I needed to take the leap.

And now that I've been away from Cape Harmony for almost a year, and away from Mom and Dad, my entire view on them has changed. As much as I might argue and disagree with Mom, she's a godsend.

I'm so glad I asked her to come help with Max this past week while he's on Christmas break. Handling all this alone would have been impossible. "Do you want anything, Mom?"

She shakes her head and offers a soft smile. "No, I'm okay. Wait, actually, if they have anything that resembles coffee, get me a cup."

I chuckle and shove my feet back into my four-inch stilettos. Definitely not the right shoes to be traveling in. "I'll see what I can find, but I'm not holding out much hope they have a Starbucks around the corner."

She laughs and leans over to help Max with the

videogame he's playing on his tablet. "I'll call your father and let him know what's going on."

"Good idea." I grab my purse from the empty chair next to me and make my way over to the vending machines. Eating processed foods out of bags is not how I anticipated spending Christmas Eve. At Mom and Dad's house, snuggled by the fire with an Irish coffee sounds a hell of a lot better than the swill that probably comes out of this vending machine into the Styrofoam cup.

I glance at my watch. It's only six o'clock. Maybe there's still time to get out of here tonight if the storm lets up. I scan the options in the machine, or should I say, the slim pickings. It looks like they haven't replenished this in a long time.

We'll take what we can get...otherwise, we starve.

I dig out a few singles from my wallet and insert them into the machine.

Hmmm. What are the least disgusting items?

A bag of pretzels, a granola bar, and some chocolate chip cookies. Not exactly the home-cooked holiday meal we would be having with Dad, but at least it'll tide us over, until we can get to Cape Harmony.

The ancient machine spits out my change, and my chosen items fall from their respective slots. I drop the coins into the next machine for coffee. A crappy Styrofoam cup drops down, and a brownish sludge that's supposedly coffee fills the cup. I tuck the snacks into my purse and grab the cup of coffee.

An old speaker mounted above me on the wall crackles.

They have a speaker system? Seems a little high-tech for this place.

I chuckle to myself as I turn toward the terminal.

The speaker blares. "Artemis Warren. Please head over to the office."

I freeze.

No.

The cup slips from my hand. The Styrofoam hits the ground, and scalding-hot liquid splashes against my bare legs.

I hardly feel the burn.

It can't be. Not here.

My gaze immediately slips over to Max and Mom.

Oh, my God. Did she hear the name?

Mom giggles at something Max says, and he smiles up at her. They must be playing some sort of game with the volume turned up. I scan the rest of the terminal.

Maybe I misheard. It couldn't be him.

Fate wouldn't toy with me like that.

Right?

A familiar set of broad shoulders appears at the end of the hallway that leads out to the tarmac. The man—one I know all too well, or at least, I thought I did, a very long time ago—swaggers toward the terminal in a crisp white dress shirt, suit coat, and dress slacks with a briefcase in his hand.

My breath catches in my chest. My heart thuds so loudly, it echoes in my ears.

No. No. No.

I stumble backward, desperately searching the air for something to grab onto. The room spins, and my legs wobble in my heels. My hand finds the back of a chair. I curl my fingers around it, using the sturdy plastic to keep myself upright, and suck in two deep breaths.

My lungs won't fill. My chest tightens.

The closer he strolls toward the main terminal, the more visible his familiar features become. The strong jaw. The perfect lips that kissed me senseless all those months. The strong arms that wrapped around me and held me those warm summer nights. The blue eyes I used to drown in while we stood on the beach with the waves lapping at our feet.

Even from here, they glint with the same mischievousness and passion they did all those years ago.

He glances down at his phone as he turns and disappears into the airport office on the other side of the terminal.

Life must be playing some kind of sick joke to have Artemis Warren here, in this place, with me.

What am I going to do?

ARTEMIS

"Well, shit."

I fire off the tenth email I've sent since I touched down, trying to let everybody who is important know I'm probably not going to make it to the party tonight. I've managed to keep my big announcement under wraps until now, but even knowing how much my absence is going to piss off Father and the rest of the family, I can't make up for missing the opportunity to do it on such a massive stage.

My hand clenches my phone. I barely glance up as I make my way down the hallway toward the main terminal and the office.

Why would they page me?

Hopefully, it's to give me an update on the weather. A good one. One that means I might still make it before the end of the party tonight.

I round the corner and step into the tiny room that serves as the heart of the airport terminal. The pilot and airport employee I spoke with earlier look up from where they stand behind an older gentleman, a computer in front of him.

"Did you need me?"

The pilot leans over to better see the screen. "Just trying to keep you informed. The National Weather Service just updated the forecast, and looking at this radar, unfortu-nately, we're not getting out of here tonight. They're saying at least another six inches over the next several hours."

Of course.

I scrub my hand over my face. Even though I knew it was unlikely, I've been holding out a little bit of hope that perhaps it isn't as bad as it appears. But it looks like it's just a pipe dream. "Thanks for the update. I need to make some calls and send some more emails to let people know I'm not going to be back."

The other man nods. "Keep in mind, even when the snow ends, it's gonna take a while for us to get the runway cleared enough for you to take off."

Shit. Hadn't even thought of that.

"How long will that take?"

He shrugs. "Depends." His gaze drifts out the window at the blowing whiteout engulfing the runway. "Usually, just a few hours."

Hours?

I nod and grit my teeth. These small-town airports are totally inept at dealing with shit like this, compared to major airports. "All right. Keep me updated if anything changes, please."

"I will." He flashes a smile at me. "You're not the only one stranded here, and I'm sure everybody's keeping an eye on things. I feel bad for anyone else here on Christmas Eve."

While all I'm missing is a pretentious party with snooty Manhattanites and a few relatives who only want one thing from me, other people may be missing some needed and wanted time with their families.

I huff out of the office, and the tinkling laughter of a child draws my attention to a small boy and a woman seated facing away from me on the far side of the one-room terminal. He can't be more than five or six, though, at least from here, the woman looks a little old to have a child that young.

My heart aches for him. He's going to be spending Christmas Eve here instead of wherever they were headed when the storm hit.

I run a hand through my hair and head for the row of chairs on the opposite end of the terminal from the boy. There's no need for them to overhear the angry phone calls I have to make. Their Christmas is already bad enough.

Before I dive head-first into all the shitty calls, I dial the one person who may have even a modicum of sympathy for me.

He picks up after one ring. "What have you done now, you screw up?"

I can't help but laugh. Mostly because he doesn't know how accurate that question is.

"Is that any way to greet your big brother, especially on Christmas Eve?"

Archimedes, the middle Warren child, and the closest thing I have to a best friend, chuckles. While he understands the years of pressure I've been under since taking on a bigger role in the company, he doesn't pity me. In fact, he'd be happy to man the helm. The way he sees it, being born the second son in the Warren family, might as well mean being born into obscurity.

He sighs deeply, and I can picture him reclining in his leather chair with his feet propped up on his desk. "Dad is losing his shit over here. Says you got yourself stuck in some shithole little town in Tennessee. Is it true? You won't make it tonight?"

Resting my elbows on my knees, I look down at my feet. The once perfectly shiny black leather has lost a bit of its luster—scuffed and water-spotted from the ordeal they've already endured.

Like me.

"Yeah, seems it's only getting worse from here. I'll be stuck in this airport for a while."

"Well, that sucks for you. I, however, intend to get some drinks in me and schmooze with every available social climber at the party. Guess I should say thanks for fucking up. My dance card just got fuller."

I bark out a laugh. No doubt baby bro will be out for every number he can get. He's never been serious about anyone in his life and has no plans to settle down anytime in the near future. He'd much rather spend his time jumping from bed to bed of the biggest players in town, hoping one will help him find a way out of my shadow.

"Well, it's only because they'll settle for the second-best Warren son."

Archie's laugh flows through the line, easing just a bit of the tension this day has unleashed. "Touché, big bro, but still, the old man is going to lose his shit over this. You should have left earlier. You know how he is. God forbid you fuck up Father's plans."

His aren't the only fucked-up plans.

"I know, but it is what it is, Arch. This is out of my hands."

And it was Father's fault I was flying and got caught in the storm in the first place. The meeting in Atlanta was *his* idea. Another hostile takeover of a small, family-owned company that was just looking for a little financial backing. Instead, they lost what had been run for the last hundred years by earlier generations to Father's greed.

"I can't believe you're going to leave me alone with the vultures…and Athena. You know they're making her fly home from Berkeley for this?"

Ugh.

"I know. There's no way they'll miss an opportunity to

show her off and brag, even if it means she'll miss work at her internship."

"So true. And she'll be in a shit mood all night because of it. You know they'll try to pawn her off on me without you there."

He's right. They will. Because no one else in the family but us can reel her in when she gets difficult.

"You'll enjoy it."

He barks out a laugh. "You asshole. All right, Art, I have to go. As much as I'd love to continue giving you hell, the Town Car will be here to take me to the party in a few minutes. Good luck with the fallout, buttercup."

I laugh. "You're such a shit, Archie. Be safe and Merry Christmas."

"I do what I can. And Art, Merry fucking Christmas to you, too."

He hangs up, and I recline in the seat, running my hand through my still-damp hair. I dread making these calls. But I still have more than half the damn family to get in touch with. Even though Father has undoubtedly told everyone, it's expected and the "proper" thing to do to make the calls personally and apologize for my absence.

Just one of the many reasons I was looking forward to what I was going to do tonight.

My plans are well and truly fucked.

Now, what the hell am I going to do?

CHAPTER 3

PENELOPE

I dry heave over the toilet in the tiny airport bathroom for the eighth time.

This can't be happening. What the hell is Artemis Warren doing here?

The one man who could ruin everything I've worked so hard for is at this shithole airport with me. And Max…

What did I ever do to Karma to piss her off so badly? Did he see me before I managed to duck into the bathroom? Did he see Mom and Max?

My stomach turns again, and I gag, but there's nothing left to come up.

I have absolutely nothing left. I crash onto my ass on the cool, cracked tile floor and drop my head back against the wall. It's almost exactly the same position I found myself that morning…the morning I found out I was pregnant.

The irony of the situation is not lost on me, and I let out a mirthless, slightly psychotic-sounding laugh that echoes in the bathroom. It comes across as unhinged, even to my own ears.

So, so bad. This is so, so, so bad.

It's a disaster of epic proportions. The Hindenburg and Pearl Harbor all rolled into one.

I need to get Mom and Max and get out of here. Maybe we can rent a car and drive home. It can't be more than six or seven hours to Cape Harmony. Mom and I can switch off driving and go straight through. We could spend more of Christmas Day with Dad. Or maybe there's a hotel nearby where we can hide out until the storm passes and Artemis is gone.

Neither plan is perfect, but either one will serve my purposes. All that's important is getting away from Artemis before he figures it out and ruins everything.

I suck in a deep breath and rise on shaky feet. My hand quivers as I grab my purse from the hook in the bathroom stall, dig for a mint, pop it into my mouth, and push out the swinging door.

Tiny clicks of my heels on the tiles break the eerie silence of the small space, but it doesn't remove the ominous weight sitting on my shoulders.

Splashing cold water onto my face doesn't help much, either. The red rings around my eyes, splotchy skin, and quivering lips all still remain. I'm a mess. And it shows. Anyone who sees me will know I'm having a total meltdown.

And here I thought I had become a strong, independent woman. One capable of being a single mom who handles climbing the ladder to a high-powered career.

How could I have been so wrong about myself?

One brief glimpse of that man, and I fall apart like a hormonal teenager.

I run a shaky hand through my hair and try to straighten

it before I prepare to step out and potentially face my worst nightmare wrapped in a five-thousand-dollar custom suit.

And damn, does he look good in it.

He always looked good in everything. But back then, it was mostly board shorts and nothing else on the beach. The teenage boy ready to head off to college has turned into a powerful man, every bit as I pictured he would while under the watchful eye of the Warren clan.

They were never going to let him be anything other than a clone of his father and grandfather. Another Warren lawyer and politician. Another Warren to take the helm of Warren Enterprises Worldwide. Another Warren to ensure their name and power never disappears.

He was full of hope and empty promises back then. A boy who said he could break away from the pull of that kind of power and responsibility. But, when it came down to it, he fell right in line.

Like I knew he would.

I swipe away the tears trickling down my cheeks and suck in a deep breath.

Calm, Pen. Don't scare Max.

All I need is a few minutes to gather myself and formulate a plan. And Kristy can help. After twenty years of friendship, she knows me better than anyone and will understand my panic. Her calm, rational approach to things is exactly what I need right now.

Because God knows, I am neither calm nor acting rational. I can't with Artemis in my orbit.

I fish my phone out of my purse and tap the screen until I find her number.

Please answer.

"Hey, Pen. You make it to your parents' already?"

Crap, I never let her know we had to land.

"We actually got caught in a storm and are stranded in the

middle of nowhere. Our plane has been grounded." I lean back against the sink, and my legs tremble like a newborn baby deer. At this point, I don't trust them to support me.

"Oh, Pen, that sucks. Can you get out of there? Rent a car or something? Poor Max. What about Santa?"

What about Santa, indeed...

I sigh, the list of my failures as a mom flashing before me.

But Santa is the least of my worries. "All of that just...sucks, but it isn't the most important thing at the moment."

Her laughter trickles through the line. She doesn't know the severity of my situation yet. "What could be worse than Santa not showing up for a five-year-old child? That's pretty awful. Is there a souvenir shop where you could pick up a few presents for him until—"

"Artemis Warren is here, trapped with us in this airport."

A long silence greets me from the other end of the line.

"Kristy? You there?"

"Uh, say what now? Artemis is *there*?"

"Yep. What are the odds?"

Kristy's squeal blares through the speaker. "Oh, my freaking God, Pen! Does he know you're there?"

I swipe away an errant tear. "He hasn't seen me yet; I don't think. I'm hiding in the bathroom."

Like a coward. Like I'm the one who's done something wrong when it's really Artemis who got us in this situation to begin with.

"But you saw him? You're sure it's him?"

"Oh, it's him. They called his name over the intercom. It is most *definitely* him."

A vision of him strutting through the airport, like it was his own personal runway, flits through my head.

God, he's so freaking hot.

All hard lines, chiseled jaw, muscle, and man.

I bet he still has those washboard abs, too. The bastard.

"Is he fat? Bald? Did he grow a wart on his nose?"

I chuckle.

If only.

Kristy always knows how to get me out of my own head.

"I wish, but no. He's just a handsome as ever. More so, if that's even possible. What in the hell am I going to do?"

Silence greets me again. Then…a double beep.

"Kristy? Are you there?"

No answer. I look at my phone. The call dropped.

Dammit.

The universe hates me.

I turn, drop my phone into my purse, and examine my reflection again. Some of the redness around my eyes and in my cheeks has faded, but I'm still a hot mess. "Okay, Penelope Barnes, you've got this."

Women see their exes every day, right? No big deal. Except it *is* a big deal. It's a huge freaking deal. Avoiding Artemis is top on the priority list, but just in case I can't, there's no way I'm letting him see me like this. There's no way the first time I face Artemis since that day he stomped all over my heart will be with me looking like hell.

I'll be damned if I allow him to turn me into that sad, heart-broken, seventeen-year-old girl again. I left her behind years ago and buried her deep. No way she's digging her way out of that grave.

Some things should stay buried.

A makeup touch-up helps, and I fluff my hair and rake my fingers through the long strands. Better.

Not perfect. But not the hot mess I was only minutes ago.

I adjust my dress to showcase the girls. If I have to see him, I will make him regret every damn decision he's ever made since that day on the beach.

Every. Last. One.

I slowly inch open the door and peek out into the

27

terminal area. Mom and Max still sit on the far side, occu-pied with something on his tablet. I take a step out and crane my head to the left down toward the office.

Is Artemis still in there?

If I get to Mom and Max quickly, maybe I can usher them out of here before he sees us. I step out of the bathroom fully and start to make my way across the terminal.

"Pen? Is that you?"

That familiar voice, smooth as caramel with a little hint of fire that always had me stripping off my clothes for him wraps around me, and it's like I'm seventeen again.

A shy, naïve girl from the small coastal town with no experience with men. The girl who so easily handed herself over to the boy from the big city, even though she knew he was only there for the summer. The girl who gave him her heart and her virginity. The girl who was left behind when he went home. The girl who wasn't good enough for the Warrens.

It's like the six years since then never existed.

Despite the false bravado I just conjured in the bathroom, one look at Artemis Warren...and I'm just that girl. He's just that boy.

I bite my lip to keep from screaming and turn to face the man who holds the power to destroy me.

ARTEMIS

When that bathroom door opened and she stuck out her head, the familiar dark hair and profile made my heart skip a beat.

It couldn't be her.

But when she stepped out completely, and I got a good

look at the woman emerging, all the air rushed from my lungs.

Penelope Barnes.

Penelope fucking Barnes.

Here.

Now.

Frozen in front of me in mile-high stilettos that make her impossibly long, toned legs look like they go on forever. With her back still to me, I watch her shoulders rise and fall as she takes a deep breath.

She turns slowly, and I climb from my chair on legs more unsteady than I'd like to admit.

My hands shake, and I fist them at my sides to hide my reaction to her.

"Warrens don't get emotional. Warrens are rocks."

"Pen. Oh, my God, what are you doing here?"

She plasters on a fake smile, the one she always used on other people but never on me that summer, and finally, her green eyes meet mine. "Artemis. How are you?"

I slowly close the distance between us because she already appears like she's about ready to crumble. It's the same look she gave me before she left me standing there on the beach and wouldn't let me explain. After she took my heart and smashed it into a million pieces.

And she's asking how I am?

That might be the most asinine question ever coming from her. "I am…good."

I guess?

Her eyes travel from my face down my suit to my shoes then back up. "You look good. Exactly the man I'd always pictured you'd grow into."

"Why doesn't that sound like a compliment?"

"Probably because it isn't."

Ouch.

29

That stings more than I thought it would, even though I know how she felt about my family back then. Even six years haven't softened her disdain for them.

And really, I can't say I blame her.

The Warrens have expectations. They have responsibilities. The Warrens have a code and a set of rules. I was always going to be Artemis Warren *the Third*. Grandson of a former United States Supreme Court Justice. Son of a current US Senator and CEO of one of the largest family-owned corporations in the world.

I was always going to go to law school and become a politician and head of the family business. It's what was expected of me. And I've blindly followed every rule in the book since that day on the beach.

Maybe stupidly. Maybe without truly thinking about what it had and was continuing to cost me. But I did it.

I stop my advance with a mere foot separating us. A hard gust of wind buffets the terminal, sending the windows along one wall rattling. My eyes never leave her face, though. The storm can rage outside as hard and for as long as it wants. Penelope Barnes is *here*.

Her bottom lip quivers, and her gaze darts around anywhere but on mine.

Why is she so nervous?

She's the one who walked away that night, not me.

Shouldn't this be awkward for me, not her?

I should be the one holding the grudge. The one carrying the anger. Yet, she's acting like I've harmed her somehow like I was the one who crushed *her* heart and spirit, all *her* plans for the future.

She clears her throat. "I assume you're a lawyer now?"

Another cold question. I clench my jaw and give her a sharp nod. "Graduated from law school in the spring."

"You working for your father?"

I bite back a curse. She knows the answer is yes. She doesn't need to ask, but admitting it means I went back to following the rules. I fell right back in line after our little dalliance oceanside.

The very thing we fought about that night.

"I help with his New York senatorial office and also the family business."

Her lips twist into a frown. "Of course. And how is your mother?"

I grimace and shove a hand through my hair. The disdain she holds for the woman who gave me life drips off every letter of the word *mother.* "She's well."

No doubt three drinks in by now and greeting the early comers to the party in a tight, cleavage-showing dress and draped in the most expensive jewelry Father and Grandfather have ever bought for her.

That party is all about the show. All about emphasizing how powerful the Warrens are and why the attendees should feel privileged we deign to give them any form of attention.

Pen's eyes bore into mine.

God, if looks could kill, I'd be dead a hundred times over.

Anything that was ever there between us is definitely over on her end. The love I once saw burn deeply in the evergreen depths of her eyes has been replaced by a fiery hatred.

But why?

"What are you doing here, Pen?" I glance around the terminal for a second, trying to place why she might be in this out-of-the-way small town on Christmas Eve. "Do you... work here?"

I can't think of any other logical reason she'd be here tonight. She can't possibly live nearby. She wouldn't leave the cape and her parents.

She scoffs at me and rolls her eyes. "You would think that,

wouldn't you? Do I look like I fucking work here, Art?" She waves her hands up and down her exquisite body.

My eyes trace her—the perfectly fitted black dress that hugs every curve, the classy heels she never would have been caught dead wearing six years ago, her polished and professional makeup, hiding those freckles on her nose that I love...

Loved.

So damn different from the natural beauty she sported back then.

My God, she grew up into a stunning woman.

"No, you look amazing. I mean, I just can't think of why else you're here." I spread out my hands, showcasing what just might be the tiniest airport on Earth.

Of all the places to run into her.

I've dreamed of this moment, seeing her again, so many times, it's almost surreal to have her standing in front of me now, within reach, at least physically. I've fantasized about what it would be like, what *she* would be like. I never once imagined she'd be full of this attitude and sass.

Maybe life dealt her a bad hand and turned her bitter?

I hope that's the furthest thing from the truth. I hope she's gotten everything she's ever desired since I last saw her, even if those desires no longer include me. I could never, under *any* circumstances, wish her ill. Not after what we shared. Even after what she did to me.

She sighs and blows a strand of brunette hair off her forehead with a puff of exasperated breath. "Our plane had to land because of the storm."

Our...

Of course, she has a boyfriend or is married.

I don't want to ask. I don't want to know, but I also do.

I need to know everything that's happened in her life

since the last time I saw her. The day she walked away from me and took a piece of my heart with her.

The sudden lump in my throat makes it difficult to swallow, but I manage. "Our? You're here with…"

Only I don't get to ask.

Her small hand shoots up. "No. That's none of your damn business. Not anymore."

Jeez.

I hold up my hands in surrender. "Christ, Pen, I'm sorry. I'm not trying to pry. I just…"

She taps her foot and crosses her arms over her chest. "You just what?"

"I've missed you." The words slip out before I even think of saying them.

Her entire body goes rigid. The quiver returns to her bottom lip. She clenches her fists at her sides and breathes deeply. "You don't get to say that to me, Artemis. You just don't."

The shrill ring of my phone steals the reply on my lips. I tug it from my pocket and glance at the screen.

Athena.

Of course.

I hold it up toward Pen. "It's my sister. I have to take this and let her know what's happening."

She waves a hand at me. "Take the call. We're done here, anyway. It was nice to see you, Artemis. Merry Christmas."

Pen turns on her heel and marches toward the offices on the far side of the terminal.

What the hell just happened?

My phone continues to ring. "Shit." I accept the call and run my hand over my chin. "Athena?"

"Artemis, what's up?"

Besides my blood pressure?

"Uh, nothing. I'm sure you've heard about my plight."

"Plight?" Her peel of laughter has a smile spreading across my face despite what just went down. "Don't even try to pretend you're upset about missing this party, Art. I'm hiding out in my bathroom right now, avoiding Grandmother. She's been trying to drag me down to the ballroom for an hour."

I can perfectly envision Athena sitting on the chaise in her bathroom, in an elegant party dress, probably with a bottle of vodka tucked into her garter belt. "Don't pretend you hate it so much."

She laughs again. Athena is by far the most difficult Warren child, but only because she's the one who doesn't always say yes to everything. She's the one who has always stood up to them.

I can't think of anyone else I envy more.

"I should be home tomorrow, sis. Just keep your shit together until then, at least."

"I make no promises, bro. Enjoy your respite from the family."

I'm about to say I won't, but my eyes travel to the office door Penelope just marched through only moments ago.

Maybe being stranded here isn't such a bad thing after all. This might be my chance to figure out what happened between us.

I mean, where can she go?

CHAPTER 4

PENELOPE

What the hell just happened?

It feels like I've been buried under an avalanche. I'm suffocating inside this airport. It's too small. Too closed in. There's too much...Artemis Warren.

The weight of our conversation sits heavily on my shoulders. My reaction to him...

God, I was such a bitch.

I couldn't stop myself.

It felt good.

After all these years, I finally got to show him how I feel about him. How I feel about the way he dumped me and shattered my heart into a million pieces.

Walking away from him now felt like getting back a little bit of the power he stole from me then.

Bravo for not looking back, Pen.

If I had, I might have drowned in those ocean-blue eyes again. I might have fallen into those strong arms. I might have kissed those perfect lips.

And that can never happen.

My hand shakes as I turn the knob on the door to the office. Adrenalin courses through my veins, propelling me forward.

I'm getting us out of here.

No way can I go through *that* again, or worse, if he figures out the truth... That would ruin everything.

Our pilot and the guy who held the door for us sit near what looks like a radio set up. An older gentleman glances up at me from behind a desk.

I plaster on a smile I certainly don't feel and step up to him. "Hi. Would you happen to know the latest on the weather?"

He looks down at his computer, then back at me, and frowns. "I'm afraid it's about the same. This system is stalled over us. They're calling it The Hundred Year Storm. This area hasn't seen this type of snowfall in decades."

Of course.

Seriously, what did I do to deserve this plate of crap I keep getting served?

I brace my elbow on the counter in front of the man's desk and drop my head into my hand.

Flying out today is off the table. Now, onto the next solution. It's time to get a little personal with this guy. I need answers; hopefully, he has some. I need him to help me get the hell out of this airport.

I lift my head and dig out that fake smile again. "I'm Penelope. What's your name?"

"I'm Clarence. Nice to meet you." He offers his hand.

I shake it and peek down at the photos on his desk. He's a family man. With grandchildren.

Bingo.

"Clarence, are these your grandchildren?"

He looks at an image of several small children gathered

around him in a rocking chair, and a smile lifts his lips. "They are. I have eight grandchildren and two great-grandbabies."

It's time to tug on his heartstrings. Maybe guilt will get me away from Artemis Warren.

"Clarence, could you imagine if they were stuck at an airport without a Christmas?"

His loving gaze travels over the photos. "I reckon that'd be just about the saddest holiday I could think of."

"I agree, Clarence." Time to bring on the waterworks. I sniffle to add a little something to my performance. "Do you see that little guy out there?" I point through the window in the office toward Max and Mom.

They still sit completely oblivious to the fact that my carefully orchestrated world is falling apart around me.

"That's my son, Max. If I don't get Max out of here, he's not going to have a very good Christmas. I'm afraid I've sent all his gifts ahead to our destination."

Clarence stares at Max. His lips twist into a frown as he takes in Max playing his game with Mom. The thought of that little boy not being visited by Santa bothers him.

Exactly as I hoped.

One thing I've learned over the years is that tugging on someone's heartstrings often gets you further than appealing to logic.

"Clarence, is there somewhere nearby where I can rent a car? I really have to get to Cape Harmony, North Carolina, today. It's Christmas Eve, and I will have a very disappointed son if Santa is a no-show."

He refocuses his attention on me. "There *is* a rental car place about ten miles north of here."

Ten miles. That's not far. Maybe I can get a ride out of here to the rental place.

"But…"

Of course, there's a but...

I grit my teeth and wait for the hole in my perfect plan.

"Bill and Judy went to visit their son in Philadelphia for the holidays, so it's shut down until after New Year's."

Of course, it is.

"Clarence, you gotta work with me here. I need out of this airport. Now. How do I make that happen? A cab, Uber, Lyft, anything?"

He shakes his head and offers a sympathetic smile. "No, sorry, miss. We're just a small town. None of that here."

I pinch the bridge of my nose to stave off the tears stinging my eyes. Getting out of here is starting to feel like escaping Alcatraz.

No flying. No rental car. No cabs. No Uber or Lyft. No damn way to flee from Artemis Warren and the little truth bomb sitting across the terminal with Mom.

But it's not Clarence's fault. The poor guy is here during a massive storm on Christmas Eve instead of with his family. He must have a good heart. I'm sure there weren't any plans to have this place open tonight.

I offer a genuine smile. "If you can think of anything, anything at all, no matter the cost, please let me know."

His dark eyes glimmer. "I sure will, ma'am, and I'm sorry you're in such a jam. I really am."

I just nod and sulk back toward the office door.

Shit. Shit. Shit.

I crane my head around, searching for any sign of Artemis.

He still stands not far from where I left him, phone to his ear. His head tips back, and he releases a deep laugh that carries across the small terminal. The sound hits me right in the gut. I remember that sound well. It used to be one of my favorites.

The phone in my hand rings, and I flip it over.

Kristy.

Thank God. Maybe she can come up with a plan to make it through this hell.

I swipe to answer. "Hello."

"Pen? Jeez, I've been calling you nonstop since our call dropped. The signal must suck there."

"It does." I peel my eyes off Art and walk over to the bank of windows facing the tarmac.

If I weren't so desperate, this would be beautiful. The huge flakes fall rapidly, coating the landscape in a crystal-white blanket. "I don't know how long I'll have before this call drops, so I need you to go online and look up this town. Find me anything—any rental, any car service, hotel, B&B, anything to get us out of here. I don't care what it costs."

My eyes cut over to Artemis, still on his call. He tugs at the crisp collar of his shirt. Wearing an expensive suit to work every day was the last thing he wanted back then.

Look at him now.

What happened to that sweet boy, full of hopes and dreams of his own?

The Warrens. That's what happened.

I knew they'd get their talons into him, drag him into that life, kicking and screaming. I had hoped what we had would have been stronger than their pull. But when push came to shove, he fell right in line.

Almost as if he senses me looking at him, he turns toward me, and his eyes meet mine. A small, boyish smile tugs his lips.

A memory I've fought so damn hard to forget bursts to the surface.

Mom and Dad's store. Another perfect early summer morning in Cape Harmony. The start of the tourist season when all the snooty richies from New York and the surrounding areas descend on the North Carolina coast to enjoy our perfect sandy beaches and sunshine. The day Artemis and the Warrens appeared.

The tall, dark-haired boy caught my attention right away. He swatted at his brother—who was just barely smaller than he was—for picking on their little sister. I watched them joking and playing around with each other, smiles on their faces. Growing up without any siblings, the dynamics fascinated me. They were built-in best friends.

I couldn't help laughing at them. The sound carried across the store, and those too big, too beautiful blue eyes turned my way. My mouth went dry. My breath hung in my throat. My heart and my stomach were suddenly overtaken by a swarm of butterflies.

It was instant.

Even as a teenager, barely out of high school, I knew I would love him. I knew it was something bigger than me. Bigger than him. *Us.*

It was too big. Too powerful. Too damn much for a kid to think that way, feel that way. But I let it overtake me with every shy glance we shared. Every smile. Every touch.

I knew it would be something epic. A fairy tale. One I would hold in my heart forever.

And damn if I wasn't right.

I just never imagined it would come to such a catastrophic end.

ARTEMIS

"Athena? You there?" Nothing but silence greets me. I pull the phone away from my ear and glance at the screen.

Shit. I lost the call.

I dial her again, but there's no service.

Shit. Shit. Shit.

This stupid storm. I turn to face the windows. The swirling wind pummeling the trees in the distance mirrors the way seeing Penelope again is battering my heart.

I just don't understand what happened back then.

One minute, we were lying in each other's arms in the boathouse, and the next, I was standing alone on the beach, feeling like my heart had just been ripped out of my chest.

The familiar ache returns, and I reach up and rub at the spot that still bothers me even now, six years later. With the pain comes the memory of the worst moment in my life.

SIX YEARS AGO

The evening tide pushes the waves up onto the beach, twice as far as during the day. I kick through the water, unable to stop the grin pulling at my lips. Pen and I have only been apart for a few hours, but it might as well have been a week. Each stolen moment with her in the boathouse, in the sand, in the surf, has been a gift. Every minute I'm forced to endure with the rest of the Warrens feels like an eternity. And I'm starting to suspect they're doing it intentionally to keep me from spending more time with Pen.

Actually, I don't even have to suspect. Mother told me as much when I tried to leave the dinner table tonight.

"You're not going to see that girl, are you?"

I just scowled at her and shoved back from the table hard enough to rattle the wine and water glasses. I already knew where the conversation was headed. The disdain for Penelope and the time I spent with her dripped from Mother's words. I gritted my teeth and angrily spat my reply, "So what if I am?"

She pursed her ruby-red lips together and stared me down, ensuring I could feel her displeasure. And God, how I felt it. If Bunny Warren isn't happy, she'll make sure no one else is. "What you're doing is completely inappropriate, Artemis, and you know it. Sometimes, I think you do things like this just to get a rise out of your father and me."

"Of course, you'd think that."

She's never loved someone the way I love Pen. In her eyes, there was no benefit for me from this relationship. I gripped the edge of the table harder, my knuckles turning white. Mother couldn't be more wrong.

"How dare you speak to your mother that way," Father boomed.

My red-hot gaze shot to my father.

He slammed his palm on the table. "What in the hell has gotten into you? This relationship, or whatever you want to call it, has gone on for far too long. I've allowed it to continue because this is your last summer before college. I can see, I should have put an end to it sooner. That beach trash is a terrible influence on you."

"You would look down your nose at someone brilliant, hard-working, genuinely kind, and beautiful as less than you because her family doesn't sit on a mountain made of gold."

Father rose to his feet, his fists clenched at his sides. "Artemis, that is enough! You will break this off—"

I didn't stay to argue with them about it. It was useless, and I had someone better to spend my time on. There wouldn't be any point. Nothing I can say will ever make Penelope Barnes an acceptable choice to the Warrens.

"There are standards we must uphold, son. Appearances that must be maintained. Alliances that must be solidified." *Father shouted the words so many times, I can recite them exactly.*

If they have their way, I'll be stuck in some arranged marriage to some Ivy League, uppity bitch, and walking down the aisle the day I graduate from law school.

I don't even know if I want to go to fucking law school. But they don't care about that. They don't give a shit about what I want. It has never mattered to them. I'm just a stupid, eighteen-year-old kid who's about to head off to college to start a life he doesn't even want.

But it isn't as if I have a choice. Warrens do as commanded. We toe the line. And if nothing else, I am a Warren. At least, that's what they think. They have no idea I have plans. Big ones.

They begin now.

The sand shifts beneath my bare feet as I make my way toward our spot. Moonlight reflects off the water so brightly, it's almost as if it's daytime.

My heart jumps when I see her familiar form up ahead. She's already here, waiting for me. Just like she said she would be.

It's crazy how I still feel this way every time I see her even after three months. My heart speeds up, and my breath catches in my chest at the sight of her. An entire summer is gone, yet it still feels like the first time our eyes connected at her parents' store.

She starts toward me, and we close the distance between us until I can finally pull her into my arms and press a kiss against her sweet, soft lips again. She tastes like salty air and freedom. She sags into me and returns the kiss, pouring all her love and passion into it. Into me.

I can't believe we only have one day left together before I have to go back to New York.

How can I leave, not knowing when I'll hold her in my arms again, not knowing when I'll kiss her again, not knowing when I'll feel her beneath me again?

I pull back and cradle her face between my palms. Unshed tears shimmer in her eyes, and her bottom lip quivers.

"What's wrong, Pen?"

She shakes her head and swipes away the single tear that trickles down her cheek. "We need to talk."

We do.

My confrontation with my parents earlier and my walk here have given me so much to think about. So much to consider. I finally think I know the answer to our problem. "I know we do, Pen. I have to leave tomorrow."

She chokes back a sob and abruptly pulls out of my arms. "So, you're just gonna go?"

The pain in her eyes cuts at my gut. "Don't look at me like that. I don't have a choice right now. But—"

"But nothing." She shakes her head, and tears stream down her cheeks. "I should've known. I should have fucking known."

"Known what?"

"That you would leave."

I heave out a sigh and rake my hands back through my windswept hair. "Pen...you know I can't stay right now. My parents—"

"Don't approve of me. And never will."

She's right. It doesn't matter how long we're together. She'll always be the daughter of two nobodies. Warrens don't get involved with nobodies. Warrens do things and marry people who can do something for the family. It's something that's been ingrained in us since the day we were born. It's bullshit.

"Pen," I reach out for her, "please...let me explain."

"There's nothing to explain." She sniffles and shakes her head. "You've made it very clear where your loyalty lies. And it isn't with us, with me."

"Pen, just listen. You've got it all wrong."

"What do I have wrong, Art? You're not gonna leave tomorrow?"

Goddammit.

"I have to."

"That's what I thought." She angrily swipes the tears from her cheeks as she turns on her heel and storms off across the sand.

"Pen, wait!"

I take off after her, but she spins around to face me with an anger I've never seen before flaring in her eyes.

"Don't follow me, Artemis Warren. Go back to your family. Go back to your real life. I was stupid to believe anything that happened between us or any promises that were made this summer were real. Nothing that's happened between us matters. None of this is real!"

Her words freeze me in my spot. I just watch, dumbfounded, as she turns and disappears down the moonlit beach.

"It was all real to me." My whispered words float into the ether unheard.

She didn't give me a chance to tell her. She didn't give me a chance to explain that I'd be back.

I was coming back.

For her.

CHAPTER 5

ARTEMIS

I shake off the memory and turn away from watching the storm. It only reminds me of that white-sand beach and what happened between us that night. That God-awful night when I laid my heart at her feet and she said what I felt wasn't real.

It's bad enough I'm missing the party and my opportunity not only to make my important announcement but also to talk with some of the influential clients who will be there. Clients I desperately need to be on my side when the shit hits the fan.

And the shit is most definitely still going to hit the fan.

This diversion doesn't change anything. Nothing will alter my course at this point. My plans will still move forward, just in a different way than I had initially thought.

Couple that wrench thrown into my plans with having to relive such a painful memory, and this day just keeps getting worse.

I glance at my phone again. Still no service.

Shit.

I can't even make any calls or send any emails until that comes back up. And given that it's Christmas Eve, I have a feeling that won't be for a while. If the storm knocked out anything important, it's not getting repaired for a few days, at the very least.

I sigh and slump down in my chair next to my briefcase, the weight of these missed opportunities weighing me down. I guess I just need to resign myself to my current fate. Since I'm going to be spending Christmas Eve here, I might as well try to get some work done.

It's better than reliving the most agonizing moment of my life over and over again and trying to figure out how to move forward now that I've missed my moment tonight.

I rummage through my briefcase and pull out the stack of files from my meeting earlier today. Things went better than expected. Father will be pleased. I've gained Warren Enterprises Worldwide another company, snatched it out from under poor, unsuspecting folks who just wanted help. Another notch to add to the Warren belt.

Father is as ruthless and cunning as he is attractive. It's no wonder they voted him into Congress. When he lays on the Warren charm, there's no denying him.

Or stopping him.

It's something I inherited from him, and he inherited from Grandfather. Grandfather is good, but Father is the one who perfected the technique. The one who really knows how to get under people's skin. The one who so brilliantly uses and twists people until they're so tangled, they don't know up from down, right from wrong, left from right.

I should know. He's done it to me so many times, I can't even count them. Times I was determined to stand up for myself against him and what he and Mother wanted. But I always walked out of his office after agreeing to the very thing I had been so adamantly against only moments before.

It's a skill he learned working with Grandfather and then honed in Congress.

A skill I can use, too. Just like I did in today's meeting to get what Father wanted.

I'm older and wiser than I was in Cape Harmony. More experienced. A bit harder than that hopeful boy. My eyes are open to what really goes on in the world. I no longer wear the rose-colored glasses that prevent me from seeing what's really happening.

That was one good thing Georgetown did for me. Law school and volunteering at the pro bono clinic showed me a side of humanity I'd never seen before. One that had me second-guessing everything I was taught to believe was the truth. That experience will always be with me and still rests heavily on my heart. It guides me to this day. It's what eats away at me when I have to go out and do Father's bidding.

It's one of the reasons I was going to make my announcement tonight.

And I'll still do it. That announcement will happen. I just need to find another time. Another place. Something just as public so Father, Mother, Grandmother, and Grandfather can all experience what it's like to be slapped in the face publicly. The same way they've done to me so many times, including when they made me leave Penelope in Cape Harmony.

I glance toward the office she disappeared into a few moments ago, and my heart sinks all over again. No sign of her. Either she slipped out and found somewhere to hunker down, or she's still in there, trying to find a hole in the storm to get out of here.

The effort is futile, though. That radar looked brutal. We're not going anywhere.

All we can do is sit and wait it out.

On Christmas Eve.

I scan the terminal, my gaze landing on the small boy with the woman I'm assuming is his grandmother. He looks content, playing on his tablet, but I know at that age, I would've been devastated not to be home on Christmas Eve. Poor kid is probably worrying about Santa and wondering if he's going to get any presents.

My heart aches for him.

That was one thing you never had to worry about as a Warren child. We were always spoiled and were given far more than we ever needed. We still are.

But maybe I can help make this kid's day a little bit better.

I rummage through my briefcase until my hand finds the item I was searching for. Grandmother will be disappointed when I finally get to New York, but the old woman can just deal with it. Someone more important needs it more than she does.

With the elegantly wrapped package in my hand and determination in my heart to make someone's Christmas Eve just a little bit better, I set out across the terminal. It may not be a new bike or new videogame or whatever it is little boys play with these days, but I'm hoping it's enough to put a smile on this kid's face.

That would be enough to make *me* smile this Christmas, even if my plans were thwarted, and even if Penelope Barnes *is* hiding from me.

PENELOPE

I poke my head into the terminal again to scope out Artemis' location. If he's still busy on a phone call, maybe I can get

Mom and Max to come hang out with me in the office or even the hallway while I wait for some miracle rescue.

Anything to keep our distance from him and the possibility that he'll discover my secret.

I don't know what I'll do if he uncovers the truth.

Run? Hide? Move? All of the above?

Luck has done me wrong again because Artemis isn't tied up on his phone. He's halfway across the terminal, walking straight toward Mom and Max.

My worst fear is coming to life before my eyes.

Just when I thought this day couldn't get any more hellish...

No. No. No. No.

One of the most powerful men from one of the most influential families in the country is about to discover my deception. He's about to unravel the truth that will destroy the life I've worked so hard to create for Max.

I need to stop him.

Now!

I dart out of the office and around chairs, on a course to intercept him. My legs barely support my weight. My heels wobble under my feet, not designed for a sprint. I cry out his name in sheer desperation, "Artemis!"

The world stands still as he freezes in place, only a few steps shy of reaching his target. He slowly turns to face me.

But it's too late.

I already know what he will see. My secret is about to be out. My carefully structured world about to be undone.

Mom glances up at the familiar name. "Artemis Warren?"

Her shocked, too quiet, quivering voice sounds panicked even to my ears. She focuses on him, then darts her gaze to me. I can see the gears churning. She's trying to formulate a plan to diffuse the situation, to help me like she always has. Or, maybe she's searching for a means of escape.

Too bad there isn't one.

I'll do anything to stop the next few moments from happening.

Anything, but it's pointless. I just shake my head in disbelief, tears stinging my eyes. All the years of hard work to give us, *him* a better, safer life...*gone.* Just like that.

Nowhere to go, Mom. There's nowhere left to run.

Artemis glances between Mom and me. "Mrs. Barnes? Is that you?"

A smile spreads across his face looking at her until his eyes drift down to Max, where he's nestled on her lap.

My world stops spinning.

Max stares up at Artemis with an eyebrow raised. He examines the man standing in front of them with calculating eyes. Ones he shares with his father. Eyes that have haunted my dreams, my reality, my nightmares for over half a decade. "Are you a friend of my mom?"

It's like watching a train wreck in slow motion. I can see it barreling down the track toward the car stuck at the crossing, but there's nothing I can do. There's no way to divert it. No way to stop the impending disaster.

Artemis' eyes narrow on Max, and I can almost see the questions and calculations running through his head.

This is it. This is the moment I have dreaded since I walked away from him on that beach.

That summer. That shitty, wonderful, life-altering summer.

This moment will change everything. For all of us.

Forever.

Artemis straightens, and he clears his throat before he approaches Max and Mom. He squats down in front of them and pauses a moment, no doubt to muster up that ingrained Warren composure.

"Hello, Jolynn." He doesn't even look at Mom.

She doesn't matter right now. Nothing or no one else does at this moment.

His eyes never leave Max. "I'm an old friend of your mom's, buddy, and I have something for you."

He hands Max a small, immaculately wrapped box.

Max's eyes widened, and he grins. "For me?"

Artemis nods. "Merry Christmas…."

He trails off and glances at Mom, patiently waiting for her to fill in the name, but I know underneath that calm exterior, a storm rages. A storm that would make this Hundred-Year Storm pale in comparison.

She swallows thickly, and her gaze darts to me, seeking approval. There's no way around it at this point. There's no way to hide the truth. She knows it as much as I do. The truth is literally staring right at him.

I give her a small nod, and hot tears spill down my cheeks.

God, he is going to hate me.

With a forced smile, she clears the nerves from her throat and focuses on Artemis. "Max. His name is Maxwell."

Artemis almost falls over but manages to reach out and grab the chair next to Max to steady himself. He pushes to his feet and turns to face me while Max tears into the wrapping paper.

A gleeful smile crosses Max's lips. "Wow! Chocolate!"

My heart pounds against my ribs. This is it. My world is crumbling to ashes around me at this tiny, piece of shit airport. I can't drag my gaze from Art's. I can't even be concerned about the amount of sugar that's probably in those damn things Max is shoveling into his mouth.

Not when Artemis is staring at me with accusation and hellfire in his eyes. "Penelope. I think you and I need to have a little chat."

CHAPTER 6

ARTEMIS

I knew it the second he looked up at me. Even if Penelope and Jolynn hadn't been here, even if I would have run into the kid out on the street or in a mall somewhere, I would've known, without a shadow of a doubt, that he was mine.

My son. I have a son.

Every childhood picture flashes before my mind's eye. It's like looking into a mirror at that age. The same blue eyes I see every day look up at me from underneath long, dark lashes and floppy, dark hair.

My hair.

There's no denying he's a Warren. There's no more hiding the truth. And the name that she gave him...my middle name. She couldn't name him Artemis. No, that would've been too obvious. That would have raised too many questions. Especially from anyone who knew my family and me when we vacationed there that summer. Which was pretty much everyone.

It was a nod to me without being blatant.

I'd find that almost endearing, sweet, heart-warming even if it weren't for the fact that she's kept my son from me for all of these years.

Years...fucking years I've missed with my son.

His birth, first steps, first words, everything. I've missed everything.

Why would she do this? How could she do this?

It's like I never really knew her at all. The Penelope I fell in love with that summer would never make the decision to keep my son from me.

The revelation shatters my heart, and I didn't even think that possible after what she did to it that day.

Shit.

That night on the beach.

She knew!

Penelope stares at me with wide, watery eyes. Tears stream down her beautiful face. A face I have loved from the moment I saw her all those years ago. Fear darkens the normally light-green irises, and her lip quivers.

She's scared. She should be.

She was pregnant and didn't tell me...

I have a son, and she kept him from me...

I clench my fists at my sides and step toward her.

Jolynn clears her throat. "I need to use the bathroom. Maxwell, come with me. We can explore a little bit."

Good call, Jolynn.

This could get ugly. Very ugly.

I glance over my shoulder at them. Max has already torn into the box of chocolate originally intended for Grandmother, and his mouth is so full, he looks like a chipmunk stockpiling for winter.

He mumbles what I think is an agreement to his grandmother, and she reaches out and takes his hand. He sets the box on the chair and allows her to lead him toward the bathrooms on the other side of the terminal.

I barely manage to tear my eyes from him, afraid Jolynn may leave with him. As irrational as that fear may be, it's there all the same. They have kept him from me all this time.

Penelope wavers in her mile-high stilettos and grabs the back of a chair to steady herself.

I run a hand over my face. I'm afraid to hear the answer, but I need to ask the question. "Were you ever going to tell me?"

She shakes her head and bites back a sob. "Honestly? No."

My heart breaks a little more.

How can she hate me this much?

Two steps bring me close enough to her to feel her body heat and for her to experience the anger rolling off me. "Why the hell not, Pen? He's my son. I had the right to know. I have the right to—"

"To what? Be involved in his life?" She crosses her arms over her chest and barks out a sardonic laugh. "If you had known about the baby, if your *parents* had known about the baby, one of two things would've happened. Either they would've somehow forced me into having an abortion, or they would have paid me off to stay quiet about carrying your baby. A Warren bastard."

I open my mouth to argue with her, to tell her how wrong she is about how things would've been, but I can't. Because she's right. That's exactly what they would've done. I don't even have a doubt about that.

"Besides," she continues, "I tried to tell you. That night on the beach. I just found out. I was going to tell you before you left, try to give you another reason to stay. But you made it abundantly clear you were going to leave no matter what I said or how I felt. What I wanted, no...what I *needed* didn't even matter to you."

Jesus. Is that what she really thinks happened?

I take the final step separating us and grab her upper arm. "Is that what you think? Really? That I needed some reason to make me stay? That I went there to say goodbye to you?"

"Isn't that exactly what happened?"

I grit my teeth. I'm *this* close to coming completely unhinged. "Yes, but only because you wouldn't listen to me. You wouldn't let me talk to you, wouldn't let me tell you what I wanted to say. To tell you what *I* wanted. Which was, that maybe my family didn't think you were good enough for me and didn't want me to be with you, but that I didn't give a single fuck what they thought. That I was ready to go home with them, pack up whatever they would let me take with me, and leave the Warren compound to come back to *you*."

Her eyes widen, and she wavers again, my hand on her arm the only thing keeping her from falling. "No." She shakes her head. "No, no, no. Don't you dare try to pull this shit on me now, Artemis."

"What?"

She sets her shoulders and stares me down. "I'm not some jury you can charm, and I'm not some young, naïve girl standing on the beach anymore. I've had to step up. I've had to raise that boy alone, support him while trying to create a career for myself, a future for him, a life for us."

I squeeze her arm, maybe a little too tightly. "You didn't *have* to raise him alone. I would've been there in a heartbeat, for both of you. If you'd only *let* me."

PENELOPE

I wish I could believe him. I wish I could truly trust that he would've given up everything the Warren name stands for in order to be with our son and me.

God, how I want it to be true.

But I can't. I don't.

Not then. Not now.

I drag my eyes away from his and look down his suit to his feet then back up. "That's bullshit, Artemis, and we both know it. Look at you. You're the spitting image of your father. And what I imagine your grandfather looked like fifty years ago, too. The very definition of a Warren."

His jaw tightens, and a muscle there tics. I'm rattling him, but I'm not done yet. Not by a longshot.

"You let me walk away on that beach, and you went home and became exactly what they wanted from you. You didn't stray one iota from the plan that they laid out for you when you were still in your mother's womb. A bastard child with some white-trash girl from North Carolina would have messed up everything. For you, for your family…Max and I would've been nothing more than your dirty little secret."

I suck in a deep breath because now that I've opened the dam, there's no stopping the flood of things I've wanted to say for half a decade. The hurt I've kept bottled up for years threatens to choke me, but the words keep coming.

"Don't pretend we would've been some happy family because we both know it's a lie. You never called, not once after that day. I wasn't even a blip on your radar after you last saw me. I was nothing more to you than a way to pass your summer. I wasn't good enough for you, for your family, and I never will be. We aren't good enough for the Warren legacy."

He releases my arm, takes a step back, closes his eyes, and shoves his hand through his hair angrily. He turns away from me for a moment, and it gives me a second to try to regain a little composure after my verbal diarrhea.

I have imagined how this would go down a million times over the years. I pictured how Artemis would react to finding out he had a son. And in every single one of them, he went straight into Warren mode.

It's one of the main reasons I kept this from him all these years. He will never walk away from his own child, but there's also no way he will go against his family and their plans for him. And even though Max may be an embarrassment, the Warrens will want to keep him under wraps. They will find a way to sink their claws into him and into me. He is a Warren heir, after all, bastard or not. I wouldn't put it past that family to try to buy me off. Offer me money for silence. Money for schooling. Money to ensure we never go public with who Max is.

As if I would ever do that in the first place...

They can make my life a living hell. Their money and their reach know no end. I want Max as far away from the hooks of the Warrens as he can get. My sweet, generous, selfless son is not going to become a greedy, corrupt, bloodsucker like the rest of them. Like the man standing before me. I will never allow that to happen.

Never.

Blood thrums in my ears and burns in my veins. The more I think about what the Warrens mean for Max, the more committed I am to keeping him safe from them.

His life will never be the same. Neither will mine.

My legs may feel like Jell-O, but I can't let Artemis see my weakness.

Warrens prey on the weak the way lionesses pick off the smallest and slowest gazelle.

I regain my balance and straighten my spine. I'm in for the fight of my life.

Artemis opens his eyes and turns back to me. "I don't even know what to say right now, Pen. I'm so fucking angry that words seem to have escaped me."

That's a first. One thing Artemis and all the Artemises before him are good at is putting on a flashy smile and saying the right words to get people to do their bidding.

That won't work on me, though. He's not going to use his name or his power or his connections to do the thing I've been dreading since the day I stared down at that positive test. He's not going to take Max away from me.

I won't let it happen.

"You're not taking him." The words come out shakier than I had hoped. With less conviction. I can't seem to muster up any false bravado. Maybe because I know if he tried, he would probably succeed. He has the ability to make that a reality.

He scowls at me and twists around to look toward the bathroom. Thankfully, Mom and Max haven't come out yet. He's never seen me argue with anyone, and I don't want him to witness this.

The man with the power to completely destroy me sighs and clenches his fists. "Are you fucking serious? I don't believe this. I can't even talk to you right now. I…"

He sighs and walks away across the terminal toward where his briefcase sits on an empty chair.

In all the time we spent together those three months, practically every waking hour, I never saw Artemis Warren, III, angry.

And now that I have, I'm even more terrified.

CHAPTER 7

ARTEMIS

People always say they see red when they're angry, but all I see is white.

White-hot rage mixing with the falling snow outside.

Everything around me is just…white.

And I don't know what direction is up or down anymore, or what is right or wrong.

How? How could she do this? How could she keep this a secret? How could she keep him from me?

Have things really changed so much? Has *she* that she can live every day looking at that boy, knowing she's keeping him from his father? I don't know shit about Penelope Barnes anymore. Maybe I never did.

That doesn't help ease the sting of her treachery. I've been betrayed by a lot of people in my life. Mostly ones I share blood with but also business associates and even women. People always have an ulterior motive. They always have something they want, whether it's the money, power, or fame the Warren name can give them.

But this…this is a completely new experience. Pen betrayed me in the worst way possible, yet her motives are what have me reeling.

I am seething, but I don't know if I can truly hate her. She may be completely wrong about what happened on the beach that day, but what she just said explains so much I never understood about why things went down the way they did.

All she wanted that night was for me to tell her I loved her and that I wasn't going anywhere. She needed to know I was committed to her and that nothing my family said or did could tear us apart. Did I do that? Did I offer any fucking assurances? *No*. Nothing. Not one fucking thing. Instead, the first thing I said was that I was leaving the next day.

I'm an idiot.

As soon as those words were out of my mouth, she closed herself off completely. She was finished. She needed to protect herself. So much so that she couldn't even tell me she was pregnant. Because she was so terrified of the Warrens and me, of the weight our family, our very name carries, and what that would mean for a pregnant young woman. The press alone would have skewered her, not to mention those who share my blood and the circle they travel in.

Can I really blame her?

The disdain they all had for her the entire summer was so obvious. I couldn't even bring her to the house for fear they would say or do something so insulting that she would never forgive me for it. They would have made sure she was as aware as I was of just how much they didn't approve of her or her pedigree.

If they had known she was carrying my child, how much worse would it have been for her? For me? For him?

It could have been so different. Maybe there could have been a way. But instead of pouring my heart out, instead of chasing her and *making* her listen, I let her misinterpret me. I let her cut me off from explaining my plan. I let her leave me on that beach and walk away without looking back.

And why, why didn't I ever call her? My precious, wounded pride and broken heart?

Look where that got us. She's had to struggle to raise him alone, no more than a child herself, and I'm here trying to wrap my head around the fact that I have a son.

I have a son. I'm a dad. I am someone's father.

That's fucking terrifying.

What kind of dad will I even be?

I sure as hell didn't have a very good example. This entire situation may be full of uncertainty and questions, but one thing is crystal clear in my mind—I definitely won't be like the Artemis Warrens who have come before me.

Absolutely not.

They saw their children as assets and used them that way. Anything that benefitted the family, regardless of how much it might damage their children, was on the table. We were paraded around without regard for our feelings or desires. Hell, we still are. The party tonight is a perfect example.

I wouldn't wish that on my worst enemy. And there's no way it's happening to my son, even if he does have Warren blood.

The door to the bathroom opens, and I whirl around and watch Jolynn emerge with Max in tow.

This is surreal.

I'm staring at my *son*. A miniature version of me, only he still has the spark of life and curiosity in his eyes. Something I lost a long time ago.

He waves at me with a smile. "Thanks for the chocolate, Mister Art-mus."

I smile, my heart practically melting, and wave at them because I don't know what else to do. I'm a complete stranger to my own child. My own flesh and blood, and he doesn't even know who I am. I need to remedy that.

But first, I need to figure out what to do. One skill all the Warrens learned while off at expensive prep schools is how to prepare for anything. Line up resources. Pinpoint timelines. Sniff out and target the weaknesses of opponents.

"Warrens must always have a plan. We must be ready for anything."

Devising an avenue of attack has always been one of my strong suits. I just never imagined I would have to use it against Penelope.

I don't want to hurt her, but if it has to be done to get my son, I'll do whatever it takes.

Her statement from earlier echoes in my ears... *"You're not going to take him."*

She has no intention of handing him over. She was never even going to tell me about him—at all. As much as I would love to believe it won't, there's a very real chance this may end up in a nasty court battle.

I grab my phone.

Please let there be service.

Two bars on the upper left corner have me letting out a breath of relief.

Thank God. A connection to civilization.

They'll all be at the party now, but hopefully, Archie still has his phone on and is looking for an excuse to duck out for a few minutes. He's the only one I can trust with this right now, the only one who won't go running to Father or Grandfather right away with this sensitive information.

I need his advice. I need his help.

Because I don't know what the hell to do.

PENELOPE

What the hell do I do?

Every inch of my body shakes. My chest tightens. The world around me blurs.

I'm either having a heart attack or a panic attack. Either one is warranted, given the situation. Artemis holds all the power. His name alone will open doors and grant him favors.

This may be the last Christmas I have with Max, and we're spending it in this Godforsaken place.

I can't let him see my panic.

No matter what sort of drama envelops us, I won't ruin his Christmas any more than it already has been.

Pull yourself together.

I right myself and let go of the chair I've been using to keep me from falling flat on my face. It's just in time.

Max and Mom appear from the bathroom. They pause next to Artemis, and I hold my breath as Max says something to him. Artie says something back, then they leave him and make their way over to me.

I finally suck in another breath and drop into a chair next to the box of chocolates Artemis gave Max.

So damn thoughtful.

He was doing it for a complete stranger—offering a gift that was probably intended for someone else. It was one of the reasons I fell in love with him in the first place. Artemis Warren had a good heart. It's what set him apart from the other Warrens. Even though he tried to keep me from seeing the distaste and resentment they had toward me that summer, it was hard to miss it. But Artie protected me from it. He tried to insulate me from their hate. There *was* goodness in him. A piece of humanity buried under that polished upbringing and good manners. I can only pray it's still there, and he somehow manages to forgive me for what I did and not take it out on Max.

I lower my face into my hands and press my elbows to my knees. If Max sees how upset I am, he will get worried. He's such a sweet child, and I can't put him through any anguish today.

His giggle is what finally makes me glance up.

Mom drops into the seat next to me. She hands the box of chocolates to Max on the other side of her and wraps an arm around my shoulder. "How did it go with Artemis?"

I rub my eyes then peek up to make sure Max is occupied. His face is buried in his tablet, and his headphones will prevent him from hearing anything I'm about to say.

"About as well as you would expect."

"I didn't hear any yelling. I had envisioned more yelling."

"You mean, like when I told you and Dad that I was pregnant?"

That's not a day I ever want to have to relive. I never thought they'd forgive me.

The corners of her mouth turn up in a grin. "Yeah, kind of like that. It was hard for us to accept the news, but we've always supported you and Max, haven't we?"

"You've more than supported me, Mom."

Most seventeen-year-old girls who get pregnant probably think their lives are over and that all their dreams have gone out the window, but Mom and Dad assured me that wasn't going to happen to me. While my plans for college no longer included attending Duke, they assured me I would still get my degree. First at the local community college while I was pregnant and then with online courses while I worked to support Max. They ensured I still had every opportunity to follow my dreams, all while helping me take care of a baby.

And they never questioned my decision not to tell Artemis.

Growing up and living in Cape Harmony, everyone knew what it meant to get involved with someone from the city. It was never anything permanent. Just a summer fling. Just rich boys fooling around with local girls, and rich girls living out their fantasies with local boys.

Mom has spent years helping calm my fears that Artemis would find out about Max and try to take him away, and now, that exact horror is unfolding here and today, of all days.

I bark out a mirthless laugh and shake my head. "What am I gonna do, Mom? What if he tries to take him?"

We both turn and look at Artemis. He stands stick straight with his back to us, staring out the window, phone pressed to his ear. My guess is he's on the phone with his attorney, trying to figure out what his rights are and how to enforce them.

He's going to get the best custody attorney in the country. He's going to make me look like trash compared to what he can offer Max.

How can a single mom working as an assistant ever compete with the Warrens?

He can give Maxwell things I could never imagine. The best schools. The best clothing. The best opportunities.

Shit. Maybe I was selfish in keeping him to myself all this time.

All these things I'm preventing him from having could improve his life and future. But I thought what I was doing was right, for Max and for Artemis. I never wanted to ruin Artie's potential political career with a scandal. Even if I hadn't been afraid of what the Warrens would do to Max, I would have wanted to protect Artemis' future, too.

I guess even the best of intentions sometimes lead to the worst of consequences. And this truly is the worst. Not only am I confronting my biggest demon, but I'm doing it trapped in this building on Christmas Eve.

Mom rubs my back lightly and leans into me. "You need to talk to him again. When you both calm down a little bit. You need to appeal to logic. Max doesn't know him. The only life he does know is you. You need to explain what it would do to Max to take him away from everything he knows at this age."

She's right.

Deep down, I know she's making sense, but right doesn't matter now. Not when my worst nightmares are coming true.

Does it?

If they take Max away, I don't even know what I would do.

I will fight if they try to take him, but no one stands against the Warrens and comes out unscathed on the other side.

"I would love to believe that will work, Mom, but this is the Warrens we're talking about. They have more power than sense. And I fear Max is just going to become another pawn to move around in the chess match they call life."

She grabs my face and turns it until I'm looking at her eyes. She wipes a tear from my cheek. If this had to happen, I am so thankful she's here.

"Penelope, remember that you're the queen, and he's just the king. You hold all the power on this board, not him."

CHAPTER 8

PENELOPE

I gently run my fingers through Max's soft, dark hair where his head rests on my lap. The light, rhythmic sound of his sleeping breaths somewhat helps soothe the tension that's plagued my body since the moment I heard that name over the loudspeaker.

He's safe. He's happy. He's here with me right now. He's sleeping peacefully.

I'm surprised Max is able to sleep after all the sugar he ingested. The half-eaten box of chocolates still sits on an empty chair next to me. We managed to stop him before he consumed the entire thing, and we made him eat the least *unhealthy* things we could find from the snack machines, but it was still far from the ideal Christmas dinner.

My poor, sweet boy. What will happen to us?

Despite his ability to remain oblivious to the drama surrounding him, I can't forget another showdown is coming.

Mom sips cautiously at her second cup of sludgy coffee

while we continue to watch Artemis pace near the windows across the terminal. He's been at it for hours, occasionally glancing our direction but giving no indication about what he's thinking or doing.

The man is infuriating. Leaving me hanging like this, letting me wonder if he's going to try to take my child on that plane with him when he leaves tomorrow.

My chest aches at the thought, and I tighten my hold on Max.

I couldn't bear it.

Mom leans closer to me. "If you squeeze him too hard, he might pop." She grins at me, and I return it even though I'm not feeling any humor in the situation.

What do I do if he actually tries to take him? How do I stop him? Could I if I tried?

"You need to stop thinking the worst, Pen. Give Artemis some credit and wait until you know more before you jump to conclusions about how he'll proceed."

"Since when are you suddenly the head of the Artemis Warren fan club?"

She laughs and shakes her head. "I'm not. I just don't like seeing you so distressed, and you know my motto, 'don't worry until there's something to worry about.'"

"Yeah, yeah, yeah." I swallow thickly as Artemis slips his phone into his pocket and turns toward us. "Well, something to worry about is heading this way."

Artemis approaches us slowly. Each step he takes ratchets my heartrate up ten notches until it's racing so hard, my ribs actually hurt. His gaze drifts down to my lap, and a tiny smile tugs at his lips.

Mom grabs a magazine from my briefcase and moves over to another set of chairs a few feet away.

Way to flee when things get dicey, Mom.

Artemis stops in front of me and stares down at Max. He motions toward the seat Mom just vacated. "Can I sit?"

"That depends."

One of his dark brows arches. "On what?"

"On what you want from me." I nod down toward Max. "From him."

The only man I've ever loved sighs and pleads with me from soft blue eyes, ones I used to drown in so easily and could so easily again. "I don't know, Pen. And that's me being honest right now."

My heart unexpectedly goes out to him. I've constantly felt a twinge of guilt, keeping him from knowing his son, but I was always able to overcome that and justify it in my head. I was always able to convince myself I was doing the right thing for both of them. But seeing how distressed he is now, puts a chink in my armor—the armor I erected around my heart the day I left Artemis standing alone on the sand.

I motion toward the seat next to me.

He slowly lowers himself down without taking his gaze off Max. "Thank you."

All I did was let him sit. That doesn't really warrant any gratitude. Maybe that's more than he was expecting.

I nod and continue to run my fingers through Max's hair.

"When is his birthday?"

It's such a simple question, but it makes my guilt claw at my stomach all the same. He doesn't know anything about his own son, even the most basic fact. Because of me. "April 5th."

Am I a monster for what I've done?

He nods slowly and watches my hand make the repetitive motion. "What did you tell him about his father?"

Ouch.

That question stings even more than the last, and rightfully so. He has every right to ask. Every damn right to want to know what's gone on in the last five years.

I sigh. "He always knew he was different growing up without a dad when other kids had one. I told him his dad loved him, but he couldn't be with us because of his job. I thought that was as close to the truth as I could get, given the circumstances."

Artemis assesses me for a second. His jaw tightens as he considers my answer, then he nods again slowly. "You never told him anything else?"

"No. He's still young, Artie. The older he got, I'm sure I would've received more questions."

"And what would you have told him?"

I shrug. It's something I've thought about more times than I can count. I never had the answers. "I would've figured it out as I went along. That's what I've been doing since the day you left town."

He leans forward to rest his elbows on his knees.

The silence that lingers between us has me squirming in my seat. There were never any uncomfortable silences before. We were always so content to just *be* with each other. So many things have changed.

Finally, he sits back and turns to me with absolute clarity in his eyes. "I would've stayed. If I knew."

I have spent years debating with myself whether or not that is true. Whether he could've given up every single thing the Warrens offered to live in a tiny coastal town, go to community college, and raise a child at eighteen. I never thought it was something that was possible, but looking at him now, seeing how distressed he is, I hear it in his voice. He really means it.

Holy crap. He would have stayed.

But what does that mean now?

I swallow through my dry throat and ask the question

74

that's been weighing on my mind for five years. "Are you going to try to take him from me?"

ARTEMIS

I jerk and twist to face her fully. Her question reverberates in my ears. *"Are you going to try to take him from me?"*

If I follow the advice of Archimedes, the answer would be yes.

Hell yes.

When I finally managed to get a hold of Archie and tell him the news, his first response was to call Penelope a bitch and to demand she give me custody. The way he saw it, she was the enemy, and there was a Warren heir, *my heir* out there in the world.

Initially, I had been inclined to agree with him. I've never been so hurt, so angry in my entire life. Not even that night, which I thought was the single worst moment I would ever experience.

She's had five whole years with him. Five. Damn. Years.

I've barely had five minutes.

Five years of missing literally everything. The most important time in a child's life. When they flourish and become little people instead of just babies.

How can I ever make up for that amount of time?

The answer is, I can't. It's gone. It's time she stole from me that I can never get back.

That thought has tears forming in my eyes. She stole so much. And I am so damn angry about it, so when Archie said to take him, the anger and hurt spoke up in agreement. But after I hung up, I stared at the storm. I watched the frozen tempest bearing down so hard on the world outside, and I came to a realization.

If I continue to face the situation with anger, it won't be good for any of us, especially Max.

What will this resentment solve?

I've seen so many friends deal with parents who constantly argue, parents who hate each other and only tolerate being in the same room to appease some sort of societal norm. I've witnessed so many kids fucked up because their parents despise each other. I don't want that for Max. I don't want him to feel our disdain and think it might be even one iota his fault. Because absolutely none of it is.

I reach out and run my fingers over his soft, pale, puffy cheek. "He looks so much like me."

Penelope smiles sadly and nods. "Oh, trust me, I know. The spitting image. I have to stare at him every day and see you."

The hurt in her voice makes me recoil. "Is that such a bad thing?"

"It was for a long time. Because you broke my heart."

"*I* broke *your* heart?" I snort and shake my head. "God, Pen, you really do have this whole situation twisted around in your head. You devastated me when you walked away from me on that beach. Devasted me."

Her eyebrows shoot up, and genuine confusion crosses her face. "Really?"

I nod and lean back in the chair, those awful feelings flooding back again despite my desire to leave them in the past. "I couldn't figure out where things had gone so wrong. How we went from planning our lives together to you essentially saying it was over and my leaving town. All my plans to come back vanished in that instant, and I went home, went off to school, did everything my parents asked, and became exactly who I was supposed to be in their eyes. I did everything to try to forget you." I sigh and shake my head. None of those things worked. Not really. Every day, I carried a piece of her in my heart. "Things would've been so different if you would have just told me."

How I wish she would have told me.

She sniffles, and I glance at her to find tears running down her cheeks.

Her bottom lip quivers. "I thought I was protecting you and him. I thought I was doing the right thing. I was young and stupid. Please don't make him pay the price for my mistake. You can't take him away from me and everything he's ever known. Please, Art, please don't do that to me."

I clench my jaw as her words bounce around my head. "I deserve a chance to get to know my son, Pen. You can't argue with that."

She shakes her head and wipes at the tears. "I'm not."

"As far as custody is concerned..." I throw up my hands. "I don't have a fucking clue what to do. This whole situation is just so...complicated. I don't even know where you live now."

"Oh...Nashville. I work for Ward Music. Aaron Ward. He's an amazing producer who's teaching me the business. Mom came down to help me with Max over the Christmas break. I had a meeting today, but we always spend Christmas in Cape Harmony. We were on our way to Mom and Dad's house when we had to land."

My eyes travel over her again. Penelope Barnes is still the most beautiful girl I've ever seen. Infuriating but drop-dead gorgeous. And seeing her all grown up, dressed professionally with her fuck-me heels on, it's hard not to imagine what it would be like to be with her now. "No time to change after your meeting?"

She bites her lip and shakes her head. Then, she grins.

"Nah, this is just how I always travel. You know, casual and comfortable."

I bark out a laugh and slap my hand over my mouth. I almost forgot about my son sleeping on her lap.

God...my son.

We both freeze, and Max shifts but settles back down just as quickly.

I lean over until my lips are a hairsbreadth from Penelope's ear. It's easy to tell myself it's so I won't wake up Max, but part of me just wants to be that close again. To inhale her scent. She still smells the same—crisp and clean, and like everything I've always wanted—and it takes me right back to those carefree nights on the beach and in the boathouse. "You always were kind of a smartass, Pen."

She turns her head toward mine and meets my gaze. "And you weren't?"

I shake my head and feign incredulity. "Me? Never. But you...it was one of the things I always loved about you."

Her cheeks flush at my words, and she ducks her head and wipes away the last of the tears.

There are a lot of things I love...*loved* about Pen, and something tells me nothing has really changed. She's still the same outspoken, happy, driven girl who wanted to achieve so many things. She didn't let getting pregnant and raising a child on her own stop her.

And instead of feeling resentment toward her over the way things went down, pride starts to bloom in my chest over what she's managed to accomplish, all on her own.

She's impressive, really.

Which leaves me in a difficult position.

Is it possible to get what I want—to know my son—without hurting her?

CHAPTER 9

PENELOPE

I want to trust his motives where Max and I are concerned. I really do, but the one thing I learned during that summer was that the Warrens can't be trusted. *Ever.* They are raised to be conniving, weaselly, backstabbing, and entitled.

Back then, I thought Artemis was different.

I wanted to believe he was different. Stupid girl.

I trusted him when he said he wanted to break away from what his family was all about and carve out his own path in this world—one that included me. But those were the naïve dreams of a seventeen-year-old.

It was all we talked about that entire summer. How he wasn't even sure he wanted to be a lawyer, let alone a politician. How he knew his father would go crazy if he tried to do anything else. That he had a plan, or at least, he told me he did. That night changed everything, though.

For all of us.

Whether he really would've stayed or not is irrelevant at

this point. The deep damage has been done. To both of us. Max has already missed out on having his father in his life for five years, and Artemis has missed watching Max grow up. That's on me. I'll have to carry that regret for the rest of my life.

There seems to be a glimmer of hope for the man sitting next to me, or at least, there was at one point. But there isn't any for the rest of that plan he once had. Those days are behind both of us, and that summer is long gone. I don't want my son drawn into the middle of the Warren empire, and I can't see a way for Artemis to be involved in his life without that happening. He's firmly planted at the center of it, poised to become the CEO of Warren Enterprises World-wide when his father retires. And who the hell knows when that might be? It could be ten years; it could be tomorrow. He doesn't have the ability to step aside.

It's what is tearing me in two right now. I can't keep Art from knowing his son any longer. I don't want to hurt him, but Max has to be my priority. He always has been. The Warren family is poison. They crush and ruin anything and anyone who stands in the way of whatever prize currently catches their eyes. I can't allow Max to get caught up in that kind of life.

Speaking of the little angel. Max stirs and sits up, rubbing at his eyes.

"Hey, big guy." I rub his back gently. "You have a good nap?"

He turns to me and frowns. His tiny pout always gets me. "I thought maybe we got to Grandpa's by now."

I sigh and glance out the window behind us. The snow still falls steadily, and winds continue to whip it up into twisting tornadoes of ice. It feels like this storm will never end.

The one outside and the one raging in my heart.

While Max was out, I saw Clarence and another employee going in and out of the office with our pilot. But no one came to offer any updates, which means there aren't any good ones.

Still stuck.

I kiss Max on the top of the head. "Sorry, buddy. It looks like the storm isn't over."

He whimpers softly and huffs. "Where's Grandma?"

I point over to where she sits in the chair across the terminal, her head fallen back against the wall. "Looks like she's sleeping, too."

So jealous.

I'm exhausted. I've been awake and on my feet for almost twenty hours at this point. The rollercoaster of emotions I've experienced the last several hours has only served to drain my energy even more. But I can't sleep right now. I can't leave Max.

A yawn gives away my desire for a catnap, and I stifle it with the back of my hand.

Artemis taps my arm. "You want to get some sleep?"

"Seriously?"

"Yeah, I'll watch Max so you can rest a little bit." He seems to know my concern without me having to say the words. His hand finds mine, and he squeezes it tightly. "I'm not going anywhere, and neither is Max. Where can I go?" He nods toward the window. "That storm means we're all stuck here in the terminal. You're exhausted and need to sleep."

As much as I hate to admit it, he's right. I'm being irrational about this. They can't go anywhere, and he's Max's father. He would never hurt him or let something happen to him.

A slow grin spreads across Artemis' lips—the one that always made my stomach flip-flop and still does—and he leans down and holds his hand up to Max for a high-five. "Max and I will hang out. It'll be fine."

Max turns on my lap to look up at me. "You sleep, Mommy. I'll hang out with your friend Art-mus."

Artemis chuckles at his inability to pronounce his name. "You can call me Artie."

The offer of a break is too enticing to turn down, and Max seems so excited about hanging out with him. "Okay. Thank you."

Max jumps from my lap and digs in his bag for his tablet. "Mister Artie, come see what I have."

Artemis grins at me and points. "I need to go see the game he has."

My chest tightens as I watch him stand, move over to his son, and scoop him up into his arms.

How wonderful could our life have been had he stayed? How different would everything...all of us...have been?

He carries Max over to another set of chairs near us and sets him on his lap, whispering in his ear.

I should probably be concerned about what he's saying to him, but deep down, I know he would never reveal the whole "I am your father" thing without us discussing it first.

It's going to take some explaining and adjustment for everyone. Especially me. I'm so used to not having to discuss Max or his needs or wants with anyone. No one else has ever had a say in his life. Things are going to be so different.

My heavy eyelids droop. I lean back in the chair and prop my head against the cool window behind me. I have a lot to figure out, but my heart and mind are so very heavy and tired.

Maybe by the time I wake up, we might just have a Christmas miracle.

❄

ARTEMIS

"And if you press right here, it makes him jump, and then you can collect all the coins."

I bend over to watch what Max does on the screen. The technology these kids have is so far beyond my old video gaming systems, I wouldn't have the first idea how to play this thing. "Wow, that's really neat. You're really good at this game."

He grins up at me, and my heart just about bursts.

Is this what it feels like? Is this how all parents feel looking at the faces of their own children? Like the entire world occupies their tiny bodies? Like they're the most beautiful things on the fucking planet? How can I already feel this way when I only just met him?

I guess it's natural. Something ingrained in humans to make them love and be protective of their child. I may have missed a lot of time with him, but I'm just so thankful I have the opportunity to get to know him now. I will take every second with him I can get.

Penelope is already sound asleep as the storm rages just behind her, outside. She must be exhausted, physically and emotionally. I sure as hell am. This little boy is a bundle of energy, and she's been doing it all alone for so long.

"So, you see, I run and run and run and then, I jump, and I get all of them, and then I win." Max leaps up from my lap and cheers, his little fists flying up over his head in victory.

So damn cute.

He's so carefree, so completely oblivious to the turmoil happening around him.

"Good job, buddy." I hold up my hand for a high-five. "You're really good at this."

He climbs back up on my lap. "I know."

I stifle a laugh.

"Hey, Mister Artie, can I have more chocolate?"

The half-eaten box still sits on a chair near Pen. "What did your mom say?"

This is the first real test of my parenting. I don't want to fail.

Max's face falls. "She said I had enough chocolate."

I figured as much. I shake my head. "If your mom said you had enough, then you can't have any more right now."

He scowls and crosses his arms over his chest. "Fine."

The pouting is so adorable, I can't even be mad about it. I remember being that age and trying to get one of my parents to override the other to get what I wanted. Smooth attempt. The kid is smart.

I tickle his sides, inducing a fit of giggles, and he squeals on my lap.

"Stop it! No tickles." He flails and chokes on his own laughter, his anger over the chocolates dissipating.

"Don't be mad, buddy. Too much candy can make you sick."

"That's what mommy always says."

"Your mom is very smart, so you should listen to her when she tells you things like that."

I grab the bottle of water I bought earlier from the floor and take a swig.

His brow furrows as he considers my words. "Do you listen to my mommy when she tells you to do things?"

I choke on the water and almost spew it across the room.

Max stares at me with concern twisting his lips. "Are you okay, Mister Artie?"

I shake my head and cough. "Yeah. I'm fine. Your mom and I used to be…" I trail off, searching for the right words to politely explain our relationship to a five-year-old, "very good friends. But we haven't seen each other for a long time."

"How come?"

"Well," I sigh. I wish I knew the answer to that. "Both of us said some things we didn't mean, and our lives kind of took us in different directions."

"But you like my mom?"

It's true what they say about children. Innocent questions that aren't so innocent or simple at all.

"What do you mean, buddy?"

"You like her? Don't you? Are you still friends?"

"Of course."

It isn't exactly true. But it isn't exactly a lie either.

Had we stayed together, things would be so different now. And I'd be lying if I said I don't still have feelings for her even after learning the truth of what she did and what she kept from me.

"Your mom and I are good friends, and I like her a lot."

"Me too." He smiles up at me.

It does beg the question, though...

"Does your mom have any other friends who are boys?"

Maybe it's not an appropriate question to be asking a five-year-old, but I suddenly find myself very concerned about whether or not she's dating anyone.

He shrugs and returns his focus to the game. "Not really. Just Mister Aaron."

Mister Aaron...

I sure as hell hope he's just her boss and not also a boyfriend. I'm not sure where all this jealousy suddenly came from, but knowing another man is spending time with her and maybe my son has some sort of animalistic instinct rearing up inside me.

"She's single."

I jerk my head up and turn toward the sound of Jolynn's voice. I hadn't even noticed she woke. She grins at Max on my lap and me.

He smiles up at her. "Hi, Grandma."

She comes and sits next to me and pats my arm. "She hasn't dated."

I turn and look at her. She can't mean what I think she does. "What do you mean, she hasn't dated? Since when?"

She nods toward Max. "Since you."

"You're kidding."

There's no way an intelligent, beautiful woman like Penelope has been single this entire time. Even with a kid, she had to have been asked out. Been attracted to other people.

She's a fucking catch.

Jolynn shakes her head.

Wow.

I've had a few semi-serious relationships over the last couple of years, but nothing I would consider worth mentioning. They were great women who I had a good time with, but none of them filled the void in my heart that had been left by the dark-haired girl on the beach.

Maybe she wanted to protect Max by not dating.

"Because of Max?"

Jolynn shakes her head with a knowing glint in her eyes. She was always so welcoming to me, even though I knew she and Pen's father weren't exactly happy about her hooking up with me.

They were the kind of parents I always wished I had, though. Supportive even when their children may have done something stupid or not what they would've wanted.

She clicks her tongue. "For a guy with a fancy degree and a perfect pedigree, you sure can be dense."

I chuckle. "How so?"

She laughs and glances over at Penelope sleeping. "She didn't date anybody because deep down, she hoped you'd come back."

"But...she ended things with me. She walked away."

Jolynn shrugs and offers me a kind smile. "That may have

been what her head made her do, but her heart has always belonged to you, Artemis, even after all these years and everything that happened between you two."

I swallow the lump in my throat and shake my head.

No. It can't be true.

She can't possibly still have feelings for me after all this time. Not after the way she reacted when she saw me. Not if she really believes I could take Max away from her. She can't possibly still be in love with me.

Can she?

CHAPTER 10

PENELOPE

I'm definitely not waking up to a Christmas miracle, just my little miracle. Small hands cup my face, and Max's chocolate-scented breath assaults my senses.

"Momma, you awake?"

I open my eyes slowly. His little face is right in front of me. Chocolate covers his mouth, and he grins.

"Max, did you eat more chocolate?"

Someone gave in to his pleas. One guess who it was.

Max giggles and presses his hand over his mouth. "Just a little, Momma."

He holds his forefinger and thumb together to show me how much.

At least he's honest.

I hug him close and push myself up into a sitting position, my back protesting the motion.

Dang. When did I get so old?

I can't wait to have a good long bath and a soft bed. Preferably at Mom and Dad's house, with Max in the room right next to me. I search the terminal. Mom naps in the chair across from me, and Artemis sits to my right.

He offers me an apologetic smile. "Sorry, he's been wanting to wake you for the last half hour. I just couldn't tell him no again."

Softie.

Max tugs on my arm. "Momma, can we go see Grandpa now?"

I heave out a sigh.

He has no idea how much I wish I could do that for him right now. He's got to be tired and bored at this point. There's not much to do here, and five-year-olds are hard enough to keep entertained under normal circumstances.

I look at Artie, hoping he might have some good news for me about our ability to flee this hell, but he just shakes his head.

Great. Nothing new.

"Sorry, Max. I think we may be here a bit longer."

He whimpers and stomps his feet. "I'm ready to go."

Me too, honey. Me, too.

The last few hours have wrung me dry—physically, mentally, and definitely emotionally. I thought that night on the beach with Artemis was as bad as it could get, but tonight really takes the cake.

Things can't get any worse.

The lights flicker. We all glance up. They flicker again, and then, the entire terminal plunges into darkness.

Great. Just great.

"Shit."

Max's head jerks around, and he looks at Artemis. "Artie said a bad word, Momma."

Even in the dark, I can see Artemis cringe and mouth "I'm sorry" to me.

He's not used to having little ears around.

I squeeze Max's hand. "I know, honey, and he shouldn't do that. He just wasn't thinking."

Artemis shoves to his feet and glances over to the office. "I'm going to go see what's going on."

I nod and pull Max onto my lap.

He clutches at my neck. "It's dark, Mommy."

"Artie's going to see what's going on."

Hopefully, it's nothing too serious. A cold, dark terminal is just about the last straw my nerves can handle. And Max is at the end of his rope, too.

Mom moves over and settles into the seat Artemis just left. "I sure hope this isn't a long power outage." She glances out the window behind her. The wind still blows snow everywhere into whiteout conditions. "It's going to get really cold in here if we don't have power."

She's right. Temperatures plunged when the storm hit, and with all the windows, the cold is going to seep in with nothing to combat it.

Artemis appears out of the office with Clarence, the other employee, and our pilot, carrying large plastic totes. They set them on the floor in the terminal, and Artemis waves us over.

I set Max on his feet and take his hand. "Come on, buddy. Let's go see what Artie found for us."

We make our way over to them. Our pilot offers a sympathetic look.

Artemis grins at us. "Hey, buddy, look at all the cool stuff we have."

He pulls the top off one of the totes, revealing survival and camping equipment. He grabs what looks like a battery-operated lantern and hands it to Max. "Press that button."

Max presses a small, red button, and the lamp flickers to life. "Cool."

Artemis hands me a flashlight. His fingers brush against

mine, and a shiver rolls through me. But it isn't from the chill in the air. It's just the Warren effect. I'm clearly not immune to it.

I clear my throat and pull my hand away. "Did we totally lose power?"

Clarence nods. "The storm must've knocked out the electricity. We've got a generator, but I'm gonna have to go turn it on. The thing hasn't been used for a long time. But it should fire up. We're gonna need it to run the heat, so we need to keep the lights off. Don't know how long this might last."

That isn't exactly comforting, but at least we'll have heat for the time being.

Artemis grabs several blankets, a few large candles, and a box of matches. "We'll still have light. It'll be like we're camping."

Max jumps up and down with the lantern in his hands. "I've never been camping."

It's not exactly my scene. But seeing his excitement now makes guilt eat at my stomach. I should have taken him.

There are a lot of things that, looking back now, I should have done. If he'd had his father in his life, he might have been able to experience all those things.

Artemis squats in front of Max. "We'll go camping sometime, buddy."

I don't know whether to be terrified or relieved that he's making plans with his son. I always wanted Max to have a father. I always felt like I was depriving him of something wonderful by not letting him get to know Artemis, but all the reasons to keep him away always outweighed that. Now, seeing how good Artie is with him, I want Max to experience it, but the fear I may never see him again starts clawing at my chest.

Clarence and the other employee grab two big flashlights,

and Clarence points toward the doors to the tarmac. "We're gonna go work on the generator."

Our pilot grabs a blanket and a flashlight and nods back toward the office. "I'll keep an eye on the storm in there. We've been listening to the weather radio, too. Sounds like it might let up by dawn."

Great. Maybe I can still get to Cape Harmony for Christmas dinner.

Max races over to Mom and jumps on her lap. He holds up the lantern, and she leans down to whisper something to him.

Artemis shifts closer to me. "I saw that look on your face."

"What look?"

"When I told him I would take him camping."

I sigh and chew on my bottom lip. "I don't know how to do this, Artie. He doesn't even know who you are."

His jaw tightens, and determination darkens his eyes. "He will."

My hands shake, and I clutch them to try to hide how scared I am. I can't let Artie see it. "How do we tell him?"

"We can't until we figure this out."

Neither of us wants to say the unspoken words. That coming to some sort of agreement is going to become an issue.

We just need to get through this night. Then, we can figure everything else out.

He hands me the candles and matches, then wraps his hand around my bicep and leads me across the terminal toward Mom and Max. He points to a chair a few feet over from them, and I drop into it. Artemis pulls his hand away. I immediately miss the warmth.

Don't do that, Penelope.

I stare at the candles in my hand. He always had that

effect on me. I always turned to putty every time he was near or touched me. Hell, anytime he looked at me.

He wraps a blanket around me, then walks over and wraps one around Max and one around Mom. I can't hear what he says to Max, but Mom smiles up at him. He returns to his seat next to me and takes the matches and candles.

Light blazes and he touches the lit match to the candle. He leans into me. "You know what this reminds me of?"

My body heats at the memory, and a smile pulls at my lips. I look over at him to find a matching grin.

An unbidden sigh slips from my mouth. "How could I forget?"

ARTEMIS

There's no way she could forget because I sure as hell can't. The old boathouse on my parents' property was the perfect location to sneak away and never be found. They had built a new one two summers before, and the old building sat largely neglected on the other side of the compound since. The loft had been used for storage for years, and we snuck up there every time we could. Our perfect hideaway from the rest of the world.

But there was no electricity in the place, and it didn't have windows up there, so it was dark.

I wanted to see her.

Every magnificent inch of her.

So, I led her up there one night and surprised her with two dozen lit candles waiting.

The twinkle in her eyes and the smile on her face when she saw the room is something engrained into my brain. So is the way she looked in the flickering candlelight. And the way her naked body felt pressed against mine.

I've relived every single moment of that night a thousand times. Missed it. Missed her. I could never forget how she looked at me that night.

It's the same way she's looking at me now. Something I thought long-dead stirs to life in my chest. Hope. That maybe there *is* some way to fix what went wrong between us.

I set the candle on the floor so I can take her hand in mine. Instead of pulling it away, she squeezes it.

Maybe we aren't a lost cause.

If she doesn't pull away after everything that's gone on over the last few hours, after everything that happened back then, maybe her mother is right. Maybe she does still love me.

I don't have to ask myself or even consider whether I still love her. I've always loved her, and I will until the day I die. I thought it was obvious. I thought she knew, but maybe she doesn't realize how I really feel.

She spent so long believing something that wasn't true. Believing I could walk away from her. I may not have been the one who turned my back and stormed off down the beach, but I was the one who walked away. I could have stayed. I could have gone after her. I could have called. Not doing those things was the biggest mistake of my life. I don't intend to make that mistake again.

I brush my thumb across her palm, and she shudders. I lean in close. Close enough for her to understand my intention. "That was the best night of my life."

A tiny sigh escapes her slightly parted lips, and her eyes connect with mine. There's so much swirling there—hate, fear, hope, and maybe even love. "Mine, too."

For all I know, it's the night we conceived Max. The night that led to all of this happening. What we shared in that boathouse was real. It was special. It was something neither of us ever found with anyone else since then.

I push in even closer until her lips are just a hair's breadth away. If she wants to pull back, I've given her all the time in the world, but she doesn't move away. She closes the distance between us and presses her lips against mine.

It's like Fourth of July and New Year's Eve all at once. Fireworks explode as the memory of kissing her and having her in my arms comes flooding back with the taste of her on my tongue.

The love we shared back then in that sleepy beach town was the stuff of fairy tales. You aren't supposed to meet the love of your life at eighteen. Those relationships are meant to be fleeting. At least, that's what people always say.

Puppy love, my ass.

Mom and Dad thought I would easily get over Pen, and they probably believed I had. Because I put on a front. I took all I had learned from the Warrens about being the epitome of the perfect son in public and applied it. I figured out how to make it through each day without part of my heart.

But I wasn't living. I was just surviving.

And I don't want to go back to that. Not now that I'm within striking distance of getting everything I've ever wanted. Not just Penelope, but a *family*. A *real* one. One where the people care about each other and not just appearances.

Things are a mess now. Hell, more than a mess. Most people would probably think I should hate her, given what I learned tonight. But I can't. Because I will love Penelope Barnes forever, no matter what happens between us.

Our mouths move together, all the time between us falling away with every brush of our lips and tangle of our tongues.

She pulls back suddenly and presses her hand over her mouth, her wide eyes filled with unshed tears. "I'm sorry."

Sorry?

"For what?"

She glances over her shoulder at her mom and Max, who are occupied, playing with the lantern and his tablet. "I shouldn't have done that."

I lean into her and tuck a strand of stray hair back behind her ear. "Why the hell not?"

Her hooded eyes look back at me with pain and question. "Because I can't do this, Artemis. Not again."

She shoves to her feet, snatches the candle, and heads off toward the other corner of the terminal.

What the hell just happened?

CHAPTER 11

PENELOPE

I can't breathe.

Gasp.

I suck in air, but it doesn't seem to fill my lungs.

This can't happen again.

I set the candle on the window ledge and press my hands and forehead against the cool glass. My head spins.

I just let that happen.

That kiss. It brought back so many memories I thought were long buried and feelings I thought long dead. Except they never were. They've lain dormant, my casual lack of acknowledgment the only thing keeping them from coming up for air. Things I never wanted to admit to myself were true are bubbling to the surface.

Things that could crush what I've built, what I've worked so damn hard for. I've tried to move on, to create a life for Max and for me, that has nothing to do with Artemis Warren. But trying to deny how I feel about Artemis after *that* is futile.

I still care about him. Even after he left me. Even after I spent years trying to hate him. God help me, how I want to hate him, but…I still love him.

He's the kind of guy you don't get over. He's the kind of guy who is the love of your life. You don't move on from Artemis Warren. I knew it when I met him. I knew it every single minute I was with him and every painful second I tried to forget it.

I tried to tell myself it wasn't true, that nothing we said to each other, none of the feelings were real. But that kiss just proved I was wrong. So very wrong.

A familiar hand grips my shoulder and tugs me until I turn around.

Artemis' blue eyes swim with concern, the candlelight flickering in their depths. "Penelope, what's wrong?"

I shake my head and try to fight the burn of tears threatening to fall. It isn't working very well. "I can't do this with you, Artemis. Not again. It almost killed me then, and I can't go through it a second time."

"Go through what?"

Does he really not understand?

"You broke my heart."

He recoils slightly, as if my words have slapped him, then steps forward and pulls me into his arms. I bury my face against his chest and release a sob.

What are you doing, Penelope?

I told myself I wouldn't fall apart. I told myself I wouldn't let him see me this weak, but everything that's happened today—or I guess yesterday since it's after midnight—has been too much for me. It's one blow after another, and it's left me an emotional basket case.

He presses his face into my hair and kisses my head. "I'm sorry, Pen. I'm so sorry about the way everything went down. If I could go back and change it all, I would. I would change everything. I would've chased you down on that beach. I would've told you that I loved you and that I was coming back for you. You would've told me you were pregnant, and our entire lives would've been so different."

If only that would have happened that night.

They are the words I've wanted to hear for six years. Six very long years since the moment I knew I was pregnant, but the uncertainty of everything with Max won't let me give in. I can't let my guard down when it's the only thing protecting us right now.

I have to be strong for Max.

I try to push Artemis away, but he captures my face between his warm palms.

Don't look at him, Pen. If you do, you're a goner.

Those ocean-blue eyes were always my undoing. I could dive into their depths and swim for days and never tire. The years haven't changed that. They haven't changed much.

His thumb brushes over my cheek. "I never meant to hurt you, Pen. I would never, could never hurt you intentionally."

Warmth from his touch spreads through my limbs and draws forth a haze that clouds my ability to think rationally. And his words. Oh, his words. It's there again. The absolute sincerity in his statement that always made me feel so safe and content when I was with him. It's what made me fall in love with him in the first place. He was so smart, well-educated, and he was so passionate about everything—about life, about me, about what he wanted to do to get away from the Warren legacy—and I fell for it hook, line, and sinker.

And apparently, it still works on me because I find myself sagging against him as he presses his lips to mine.

ARTEMIS

I never knew how much she suffered. I always thought she moved on with her life so easily, leaving me in the dust to wallow in my own grief and anger. I believed I was the one who was miserable for so long, who trudged through life barely living, but seeing her like this proves how wrong I was. How dreadfully wrong.

Her mother's right. She wouldn't react this way if she didn't still have strong feelings for me. Whether they're love or not is another question. There are too many tangled emotions between us to know anything.

She's not the only one struggling to untangle the web.

The woman kept my son from me, and that's not something I can just forget. It's the ultimate betrayal, and there are so many things unsaid and undecided. But in this moment, with her in my arms and my lips against hers, none of them seem that important.

She presses her body into mine and returns my kiss fervently.

This kiss is different than the one we shared moments ago.

This one is my apology. For everything that happened. For all the ways I failed her. For not being there when she needed me so badly. And I hope she accepts it. Because I don't know what else to do or how else to make her hear the words and believe me.

"Why are you kissing my momma?"

Pen and I jerk away from each other and look down. Max stares up at us with his brow furrowed. The innocence of youth...

Of course, he has no idea why we're kissing.

How the hell do I answer that?

I glance over at Penelope for help. Maybe she can give me

some hint about how to handle Max's probing question. She has her hand pressed over her mouth, her eyes wide. The horror at being caught enveloped in a passionate embrace with me is too much for her. She's frozen. I can't help it. The terror in her eyes is so comical that a laugh bubbles up from my chest.

Her gaze meets mine, and she drops her hand and laughs, too, tipping her head back and pressing her hand against her flat stomach.

I kneel in front of Max. Here goes nothing. "I'm kissing your momma because I like her."

True and to the point.

He tilts his head sideways and darts his gaze between Penelope and me. "A lot of people like my momma, and they don't kiss her."

I bark out a laugh and ruffle his hair. He's wise beyond his years. And observant. "You'll understand when you're older, kiddo."

He shakes his head and scrunches up his face in disgust. "I'm never gonna kiss girls. They're gross."

You just wait, kid.

I push to my feet and grin at Penelope. "Looks like you're safe for a few years."

She laughs and shakes her head. "I hope more than a few."

Me too.

I only just learned about Max. There's no way my fathering skills are up to the "explaining the birds and the bees" level yet.

Max tugs on my arm and grins at me. He holds up a couple sheets of colorful construction paper. "Grandma says you know how to make something cool with this."

Oh, my God.

The origami.

My eyes connect with Pen's, and a pink flush spreads over her cheeks.

That entire summer, every time we were together, I made her something different. Growing up, my aikido instructor's grandmother used to sit and watch our classes. If my nanny was late picking me up, I would sit with her, and she taught me the art of Japanese paper folding.

It was something I did to create something beautiful in a world and family that often felt so ugly. And I wanted to create something beautiful for Penelope.

She had a box of my creations stashed under her bed. I never knew her mother knew about them.

I look over at Jolynn, who just grins and waves.

That woman has had a plan since the moment she saw me.

I accept the papers from Max and take a seat. "I don't know if I remember how to do this. It's been a long time since I've tried."

"I'll leave you boys to it, if that's okay with you?" I glance up at Penelope. The fact that she's giving me some time alone with Max soothes some of the ache of missing so much with him. It can never make up for it, but at least it proves she wants him to have a relationship with me.

"Yeah, that'd be okay."

More than okay.

I'll take all the time with him I can get. Every single second with him is a blessing. I never knew my heart could be so full and so empty at the same time. Learning about Max was like finding out my entire life has been a lie. It opened up so much potential for more. Yet, at the same time, Pen's betrayal felt like a massive slap in the face that took all my old feelings for her and twisted them into a giant cyclone of confusion.

Kissing her has only confused things more.

She offers me a knowing smile and retreats toward her

mom. I never thought I'd love seeing Penelope walk away after what she did to me on that beach, but that outfit she's wearing...

Damn.

The black dress hugs her just right in all the places that matter.

"Show me, Mister Artie!"

I jerk my gaze away from her and focus on the project at hand. The red and green sheets of paper have the potential to become anything—well, anything I can dig into very old memories and manage to remember how to make—but I know exactly what I want to create for Max.

Hopefully, he likes it.

Who knows with a kid, though?

I certainly have zero experience dealing with those of the pint-sized persuasion. This is going to take some getting used to for both of us.

I hope I don't royally fuck it up—the origami or the fatherhood stuff.

Max's earlier reaction to seeing me kiss Pen is one of the confusing things I'm not quite sure how to broach with him. The kid can't possibly grasp how complicated things are between his mother and me. Perhaps it's best to be vague and speak in generalities. Things he can understand.

"So, Max..."

He looks up at me with soft, familiar eyes. "What Mister Artie?"

"You don't have a girlfriend?"

His nose scrunches up, and he looks like he just sucked on a sour lemon. "Ewww. No, Mister Artie. That's yucky."

I chuckle and shake my head as I set up the papers to implement what I have in mind. "Like I said earlier, you won't always feel that way. One day, a pretty girl is going to cross your path, and if your intentions are honorable, you'll fall in love."

Crease, fold, crease…

Origami is like riding a damn bike. Everything old Mrs. Hamasaki taught me comes flooding back, and my hands move almost of their own volition.

I still got it.

"What are tensions, Mister Artie?"

Oh, God. How in the world do I explain this to a five-year-old?

It's not as if I'm well prepared to field these types of questions from my son. Maybe I need to do some reading. I've got a lot of catching up to do in the "Dad department."

Shit. How do I explain this?

"Well, if a man likes a woman, and he wants to be her boyfriend, then he needs to have good intentions toward her and their relationship. That means he wants her to be happy and healthy, and he'll do anything he can to help her make her dreams come true. He wants the best of the best for her."

He squints at me and considers what I just said.

Adorable.

Even at this age, he's so inquisitive and thoughtful. I don't think I was like that at five. I'm pretty sure I was a little dick. Even now, I have vivid memories of being constantly reprimanded by the various nannies who rotated through our house back then.

Max tilts his head. "What's your tensions with my momma? Are they good?"

I almost choke on my own breath.

Wow. Did not expect that.

Honesty is probably the best route here, even if Max is too young to understand it. "They are the best, buddy. I don't want anything for your mom bedsides happiness. More happiness than she can stand."

She deserves nothing less. Even with the sting of betrayal

still fresh. Even with the open wound of the time missed with Max, I can't hate her. I never could. Even when she broke my heart, I still carried a torch for her deep in my soul.

A few more folds, another crease...

There.

It's not as perfect as Mrs. Hamasaki would have expected it to be twenty years ago, but it looks like what it's supposed to be, so that's one for the win column as far as I'm concerned.

I hold my creation out to Max. "Here you go."

His eyes widen, and his jaw drops. "Wow! It's a heart!"

"Look inside. There's a surprise. The heart is a box. It opens. Just squeeze right there," I point, "on those two sides."

His tiny fingers squeeze, and the heart box pops open, just like it's supposed to. "A frog! Wow!"

A tiny green origami frog rests inside the heart-shaped box. Athena used to love them before she got too old to enjoy them. It's nice to have a new, captive audience who appreciates my paper-folding skills.

My heart swells. It feels good to pass down a tradition to my son.

"Momma! Look!" Max rushes across the terminal to Pen and his grandmother. "Mister Artie gave me his heart."

He definitely owns my heart already. He has since the moment I realized he's mine. It happened in an instant.

How do people stand it when they have to leave their children, even for a few hours?

The thought of walking away from him today, watching him climb onto a plane with Pen and Jolynn, has tears forming in my eyes.

Max drags Penelope back over to me, carrying my creation in his tiny hand. "If you squish it right here, there's a frog inside."

Pen's focus switches from Max to me, and a smile tilts her soft lips.

God, that kiss was amazing.

Now, all I can think about is when I can do it again.

"Did you thank Mister Artie for the present?"

Max turns and flings himself into my chest, his arms roping around my neck.

My son is hugging me. My perfect, wonderful son.

He squeezes me. "Thank you, Mister Artie, for the orangegami. I really like it."

I can't help but close my eyes and squeeze him back, soaking up every amazing moment.

How will I ever stand to get on my damn plane and fly away from him?

CHAPTER 12

PENELOPE

Watching Artemis with Max in the flickering candlelight has me imagining things I never thought possible. All of us spending holidays together in front of the fire. Artemis talking with Max while we wait for Santa in the morning. Going to bed wrapped in Artemis' strong, warm arms.

Even twenty-four hours ago, they were just pipe dreams. And maybe they still are. Either way, my heart is going down a very dangerous path. A path where I again open myself up to the man who almost broke me. A path where Max may end up getting hurt by the very people who are supposed to protect him.

Max's tired eyes blink slowly as he stares up at Artemis. They've been working on origami for almost an hour now. In addition to the heart box and frog, Artemis has also made Max a swan, two different flowers, and something I still haven't identified. I won't ask what it's supposed to be, though. Max doesn't seem to care that he can't identify it, and Artie just seems happy to be with his son, no matter how rusty his origami skills might be.

Artemis reaches out and ruffles Max's hair. "You getting tired again, buddy?"

Max yawns and shakes his head. "I'm not tired."

My laugh mingles with Artemis' chuckle, and he nudges Max.

I sit down next to them on the blanket. "I think you are. Why don't we go try to get some more sleep? Maybe by the time you wake up, we'll be able to get to Grandpa's."

"Really?" His eyes light up and widen. "Okay. I'll try to sleep."

That was easy. He's being so agreeable considering all we've been through today. Things are so simple for a five-year-old.

Artemis scoops him up. "Say goodnight to your mom."

Max leans down from Artie's arms and kisses me. "Night, Momma."

"Night, big guy."

He snuggles against Artemis, and the man who literally holds my heart carries him across the terminal toward Mom.

Max is already falling in love with him.

It shouldn't surprise me.

Artemis Warren is the type of guy you fall in love with easily. I sure did. We were saying the word within only a few weeks that summer, but even before that, I already felt like I had lost my heart to him.

He talks to Mom and sets Max down on the row of chairs. With the lantern on the floor below him, and a blanket tucked under his head for a pillow and another pulled over him, Max settles in for what is hopefully a long nap. This isn't the most ideal place to sleep, but this has been exhausting for all of us, the kid especially.

Mom says something to Artemis that makes him grin, and

he glances over to me. She denied being on Team Artemis earlier, but the longer this night goes on, the more I start to think she's absolutely thrilled that we're stuck here with him.

While Mom and Dad never particularly liked Artie, it wasn't because of how he treated them or me. It was his family—the same reason I'm so reluctant to believe we're capable of working things out in an amicable fashion now.

He crosses the terminal with a look I recognize all too well in his eyes. Each step he takes winds me tighter with anticipation. That look has goose bumps breaking out across my skin and heat flooding to a place that hasn't stirred to life in a very long time.

Artemis Warren is up to something, and there's something very dirty on his mind.

Oh, God. Here we go.

I can't say I blame him. That kiss earlier sent my body spiraling and has me questioning everything. It's only natural for him to be feeling the same way I do...like anything might be possible here in this terminal.

He finally pauses in front of me and stares down with warm eyes swimming with desire. "You were right. He's exhausted. He was probably already asleep by the time I got over here."

I chuckle and glance over at Max—anything to avoid looking into Artemis' heated gaze. He can see right through me to the heart of what I'm feeling, of what I want. "This has been a lot for him. A lot of excitement. A lot of new things."

He nods and holds out a hand to me.

It's such a simple gesture that holds so much meaning. The first time he took my hand in his, I was lost to him.

Can I afford to go there again?

I raise an eyebrow at him. "What are you doing?"

He flashes me that Warren grin guaranteed to melt away any reservations I have. "Trust me."

That's the ultimate ask, isn't it? For me to trust him.

I trusted him once, and I ended up alone and pregnant with a broken heart. But after everything he's said today, after all the truths that have been revealed, can I really deny that I still have feelings for this man? That he doesn't still make my heart race faster than a horse at the Kentucky Derby? That I don't still dream of him almost every night? What it was like to be in his arms. What it was like to completely lose myself to him.

They were the happiest moments of my life.

I reach out and offer my hand. His warm palm envelops mine. He squeezes and pulls me up to my feet.

"What are we doing, Artemis?"

The only answer he offers is a grin and a nod toward a small hallway to our left that I haven't even noticed before.

He glances back at Max, still unmoved in his position, and Mom, who is occupied with a magazine. "Somewhere a little more private where we can talk."

Talk. Good. We need to.

We have to figure out what's going to happen when the snow stops falling. We need to know what we're going to do about Max.

As of now, we've established exactly zero.

He grabs the candle and leads me down the short hallway, past a closed door, and into a dark corner. He sets the candle on the floor, and in a split-second, he spins me around and presses my back against the wall, caging me in with his strong arms.

Oh, my God.

A full-body quiver moves through me at his proximity.

"I miss you, Pen." His words spread over me like a soothing balm to an ache I hadn't even realized was still there.

He shifts closer, his warm breath fluttering over me. "I

know things are stressful and complicated right now, but what tonight has proven to me is something that I always knew deep in my heart." He cups my cheek with one hand.

I swallow against my suddenly dry throat. "What's that?"

He smirks and leans in until his lips brush against mine gently, reverently. "That the only time in my life I've ever been truly happy was when I was with you."

ARTEMIS

Penelope sucks in a deep breath and shivers at my words. I step closer and press the full length of my body against hers. My dick stirs to life sandwiched between our warm bodies, remembering all the wonderful times we spent together that summer.

It was the only time I could forget the world, forget who I was, forget all that was expected of me, and just live.

"Artemis—"

I silence her with a kiss—soft and earnest. She groans and shifts her body against mine, rubbing against my cock and dragging a moan from my lips. "It's been too long since I've felt you like this, Pen."

This is what it's supposed to be like. I can't even put into words how this feels.

How can you explain to someone who's never been with anyone else what it's like to be with people who aren't the right person?

I don't even want to think about those women. I don't want to think about how much time and energy I've wasted with other people when I could have been with Pen and Max.

All I want right now is to show her what she means to me, what *this* means to me, and that whatever else happens, my feelings for her will never change.

I press my forehead against hers and breathe in her familiar scent, one that I've dreamt about so many nights.

She sighs, and it's almost as if exhaling that breath releases her reservations and the tension in her body because she sags against me and wraps her arms around my neck to pull me closer. She pushes her lips against mine.

"I've missed you so much." Her words come mumbled between our fervent kisses.

We both know where this is going, and we each had plenty of time to stop it. But we surge ahead, neither prepared to end this connection we so desperately need.

I drop my hand to the hem of her dress and work it up. My fingertips brush over the warm, smooth skin of her thigh, but she doesn't pull away. She shakes and opens her legs wider for me.

"Pen…" I slide my hand up between her legs and find the thin, silky strip of her thong. I raise an eyebrow at her. The Pen I knew all those years ago would never have worn anything so risqué.

She grins. "No panty line."

Christ.

The girl I fell in love with has become such a sexy, confident woman. Just like I always knew she would. I'm so fucking sorry I missed witnessing it.

I chuckle as I work my fingers under the fabric and brush them along the apex of her thighs. She moans and clamps her legs around my hand.

God, that's hot.

I kiss her neck just beneath her ear. "Relax, baby."

She nods and releases my hand, allowing me to slip a finger into her wet heat.

"Christ, Pen. You're so wet."

The skin on her neck and cheeks flushes even darker than it already was.

"Don't be embarrassed, baby. It's hot as hell that you still want me this much. Just as much as I want you."

She mewls and squeezes around my finger. I sweep my thumb across her clit, and she bucks in my arms and clings to my shoulders.

"Please, Artemis." Her words are a plea.

I always loved hearing her beg.

Every moment we spent together back then was such a gift, one I took for granted. But even at eighteen, I knew I wanted every second of my time with her to be perfect.

This is far from the perfect location or circumstances, but being together again is as close to bliss as I'll ever find.

I press my hard cock against her belly. "Please, what?"

Say the words, Pen.

She needs to say it. I need to hear that she wants the same thing I do, no matter how stupid and reckless it might be.

I slide my finger in and out of her slowly.

Her head drops back, and she gasps. "I want you. All of you."

Fuck yes.

I growl against her ear and take her mouth in a searing kiss. Six years of pent-up need are about to be unleashed, and when they finally are, it will be truly magnificent. Just like her.

Pen reaches between us and fumbles with my belt. She manages to get it unhooked and shoves down my pants. Her fingers find the waistband of my boxers, and her hand freezes.

I tear my mouth from hers. "What's wrong, Pen?"

If she wants to stop, it'll kill me, but I would understand it. We're not teenagers anymore sneaking off to spend time alone in the boathouse—or in the back hallway of an airport.

But it isn't reservation I see in her eyes. The exact opposite.

Determination.

Need.

Lust.

Her tongue snakes out across her bottom lip. "Nothing's wrong. Just…"

"What?"

"I can't believe you're really here."

I grin at her and kiss her again as she pushes down my boxers and takes my cock in her hand. Her small fist wraps around the base of my shaft. I groan and drop my forehead against hers again. She kisses me, and I pull my hand from between her legs and lift her so she can wrap them around my waist.

This isn't how I had imagined a reunion with Penelope. Not hot and hard sex against a wall. It's certainly not what she deserves. But it's what we both need.

She positions me at her entrance, and I lock eyes with her before I slowly push inside. Her mouth falls open. Her eyes widen and then roll back as I shove in even further.

Good God. This is Heaven.

All the beautiful places I've been in my life, all the wonderful experiences I've had…nothing compares to being inside of Penelope Barnes.

She drops her head back against the wall, exposing her long, elegant neck to me. I push all the way into the hilt. She groans and tightens around me, and it forces me to grit my teeth.

The words are on the tip of my tongue—words I have only ever said to her because if I had said them to someone else, it would've been a lie. And one thing I am not is a liar. But I bite them back. I don't want to scare her away with a declaration like that when things are still so undecided. I pull my hips back and drive into her again, pushing her body against the wall.

She groans and scratches her nails against the back of my neck. I can't hold back any longer and start a relentless rhythm designed to break down any wall still standing between us.

Any barrier the past and the misunderstandings have created shatters as her hips arch up to meet my every thrust, and we move totally in sync with each other as if we've never spent any time apart and were built to be together like this.

I shift my hips slightly, and she moans loudly.

Shit.

I reach up and press my thumb over her lips. "Shh."

We're alone back here, and I doubt anyone will come looking for us. Certainly not Jolynn, the airport employees, or the other pilot who are all occupied or monitoring the storm, but just in case, I don't want to broadcast what we're doing.

Her eyes fly open and connect with mine. The normal pale-green has been replaced with the dark hue of passion. She clenches around me again, and I push harder and deeper.

She bites down on my thumb to keep from crying out as her orgasm washes over her. Her eyes roll back, and her pussy ripples along my cock.

It's my undoing.

I crash over that barrier with her into absolute bliss, emptying myself inside her. She shakes against me, then sags and drops her head forward onto my shoulders.

The words are there again, battering around in my head, combining with so many other thoughts about everything that's come to light today. The ones I can't say but I know are true, nonetheless.

I love you, Penelope Barnes.

CHAPTER 13

ARTEMIS

The lights flicker to life just as Penelope steps out from the bathroom, where she disappeared to clean up after our little romantic interlude.

I still can't believe it happened.

My heart still races, and my body vibrates at the memory of being inside her.

We may not have been smart, but doing it helped ease some of the tension the entire situation has created. Like we were both able to let go of some of the pain we'd been holding inside for the last half-decade.

She glances up at the lights, then grins at me from across the terminal.

Jolynn has thankfully been silent about what I'm sure she knows happened only a few moments ago, and until now, Max has barely moved. But the bright, overhead lights are too much. He stirs and blinks awake.

Penelope walks over to him and squats down. "Hey, buddy."

He looks around. "The lights are back on. Does that mean we can get out of here to see Grandpa?"

She settles into the seat next to me and frowns. "I don't know, but we can't leave until the storm is done and the runway is cleared."

He pouts. "I'm hungry."

My stomach growls in agreement.

Crap.

I haven't eaten anything since we landed. Mostly because ever since I laid eyes on Penelope, it's been a landslide of revelations. My gaze drifts over to the vending machines in the corner.

Pen touches my forearm. "There are a few other things left in the vending machine. Let's go see what we can find to tide us over, until we can get some real food and get out of here."

"I'll take him."

"You sure?"

I raise an eyebrow at her. "I'm perfectly capable of picking out food from a vending machine."

She chuckles. "Somehow, I imagine you've never eaten out of a vending machine your entire life."

I bark out a laugh and shake my head. "I'll have you know, I use the vending machines at the courthouse all the time when I'm hungry."

A tiny smile tugs at her lips. "Impressive. Acting like a commoner."

I scoff at her and take Max's hand to lead him over to the snacks. "What do you want to get, buddy?"

He presses his face against the glass and considers his options. "I want that big cookie and chips."

Unlikely, kid.

This parenting thing may be new, but I know those are not mom-approved choices.

I narrow my eyes at him. "I don't think your mom is going to want you eating crap. I think we should get that granola bar and a few other healthier things."

He pouts but nods. "Okay, Artie."

Another win in the parenting column for me. The kid is actually listening to me. I don't want to get my hopes up that this might be so easy with him all the time, but it makes me feel a little bit better about the situation that Max isn't fighting with me.

In reality, I'm a stranger to him, but he seems to enjoy being with me. That's all I can ask at this point, I guess.

I grab some cash out of my wallet and empty the vending machine of anything that looks even remotely healthy. Max helps me carry it all back, and we spread it out on the floor on a blanket in front of Penelope and Jolynn.

"Your Christmas feast, ladies."

They both chuckle and survey the array of sugary and salty and processed foods available.

Penelope's eyes glow with humor. "Everything looks delicious."

Max puffs out his chest. "I helped, Momma."

She smiles at him. "Good job, Max."

We all tear into the packages. This isn't how I had anticipated spending my Christmas Eve, but I have to say, things are shaping up pretty good.

I just hope when it finally comes time to make some decisions about moving forward with Max, everything stays so amicable.

Pen tosses a handful of popcorn into her mouth and glances over her shoulder toward the windows.

It looks like the storm is letting up.

A light at the end of the tunnel.

Thank God.

PENELOPE

This nightmare of a day has turned into something completely unexpected.

I can't believe I just slept with Artemis Warren...

Again...

In an airport...

With Max and Mom only fifty yards away.

What was I thinking?

Clearly, I wasn't. I glance over at Artemis as he grins at Max and holds out a piece of licorice for him.

A huge part of me always dreamed of this. Having Artie back, both for Max and for me. I wanted that, even though I was equally terrified of what it would mean for us.

It was selfish of me to want him when he would bring so much turmoil into our lives. Which is why I never let myself admit it. Which is why I never let myself give in to the desire to call him and tell him.

He was so angry earlier about what I kept from him, about what it cost him, but everything seems so different now like the tides have shifted, and maybe there's the potential to work this out in a way that we both get what we want.

At least when it comes to Max. Whether things can ever truly be okay between us is another question. I'm not dumb enough to think having sex is going to heal all the wounds.

Mom takes a bite of her granola bar and considers Artemis. "So, you're working for your father?"

I glare at her.

Why the hell is she bringing this up?

She has to know this is a sore spot for him and for me.

He chews slowly and swallows. "I am. He's getting close to retiring as CEO. His time is being sucked up in the

Senate and with political schmoozing, and he wants to focus on that and have me take over the day-to-day operations."

Mom nods and chews for a moment. "And your brother and sister?"

We didn't spend a whole lot of time with Archimedes or Athena that summer. Artemis made it clear to them that he wanted as much time alone with me as possible, and since he didn't bring me over to his family's place very often, I only met them once or twice.

Athena was barely thirteen, and Archimedes was a few years younger than Artemis. He was the one attached to their father's hip while Artie bucked any attempts from his parents to keep him in line.

Artemis picks at a piece of lint on his pants. "Archimedes works for the company, and Athena is at Berkeley."

Mom's eyes widen. "Wow, and your parents are okay with that?"

I share Mom's surprise. Berkeley isn't exactly the type of school the Warrens send their children to. Too liberal. Too California.

His gaze jerks to me. He looks about ready to defend them with some retort, but then he seems to reconsider. "Athena is…the difficult child, we'll just say."

I snort.

Athena is the difficult one?

It always seemed like Artie was the one butting heads with his parents back then, not the petite little dark-haired girl.

Mom chuckles and shakes her head. "Your parents consider a child who knows what they want to be difficult?"

He shrugs. "They do when what that child wants to do isn't what they had planned for her."

His words claw at my heart. He was so distraught that

summer about what he was being forced into. Looking for a way out. And it's exactly where he ended up.

Mom nods knowingly and offers him a sympathetic look. "I seem to recall that you weren't too keen on going to law school and joining the family business back then."

"I wasn't." His reply comes sharp and fast.

She raises an eyebrow. "What changed?"

Oh, God. Don't go there, Mom.

He glances at Max and me before returning his focus to Mom. "When things ended between Penelope and me, I made the decision to follow the original plan, which was law school and the family business."

"I see." She clicks her tongue. "So, you gave up on your own dream."

Artemis' shoulders slump. "I guess you could say that."

Mom presses her lips together. "That's sad."

It is.

And I would feel bad for him except that he did have a choice, and he made the decision all on his own. A decision that led us to where we are today...in this massive quagmire. Even if we can get things worked out with Max, I don't know what it means for us. He's in New York, and I'm in Nashville.

So, are we really going to do a long-distance relationship and try to make it work? Probably not.

That realization has bile rising in my throat.

I can't do it again. I can't offer my heart to him when he's going to walk away. Not now that I'm going to have to see him all the time because of Max.

Artemis' phone rings, and he scrambles to get it out of his pocket and pushes to his feet. His eyes harden as he stares at the screen. "I need to take this."

CHAPTER 14

ARTEMIS

"Archie, what's going on?"

I glance at my watch. Three in the morning. The party is probably just winding down about now, which means he's probably nine or ten drinks in.

It's a requirement at the Warren parties to get shit-faced. It's the only way to deal with the family and all the social climbers who come to plaster on fake smiles and kiss Warren asses.

But there are no sounds of a party in the background.

"Gee. Don't sound so happy to hear from me, Art. I talked to Marcus Benedict."

I wander over near the windows where I kissed Penelope only a few hours ago. Hearing that name erases any good feelings I had for a few seconds about the location. "What about?"

"What the fuck do you think about? He does family law. You need a family law attorney, and he's one of the best in the country."

"I know, asshole, but I thought we agreed to keep what I found out quiet until I could decide what to do."

If anyone finds out before I get things settled with Penelope, this could go downhill really fast. I damn sure don't need that.

Archie scoffs. "How can you decide what to do without consulting with somebody who knows the fucking law, Artemis?"

I scowl even though he can't see me. Sometimes, I swear he's just a younger version of Dad. And that isn't a compliment. But now, he's right. I still have no idea what I'm going to do, and, in a matter of hours, the runway is going to be clear, and Penelope and I are going to be taking off in opposite directions.

Law school taught me a lot, but family law was never on my educational radar. I only know the very basics, and I wouldn't have the first clue what my rights are or how to go about asserting them.

Maybe I shouldn't be so hard on Archie. He's only trying to help.

"Well, what did he say?"

"He said the fact that she knew she was pregnant and kept it from you is a big win for our side. He says we can definitely use that against her in a custody hearing."

"But what do I need to do to get a custody hearing?"

If it comes down to a fight in a courtroom, I'll do what I have to in order to have time with Max, but I would rather not drag them through it if I don't have to, if we can come to some mutually beneficial agreement.

"He said all you need to do is file the paperwork. The court will probably order a paternity test unless she's going to admit that he's yours."

I snort. "She can't deny he's mine, Archie. The kid looks just like me."

Archie laughs. "That means he looks like me, too. Must be a good-looking kid, then."

I chuckle and shake my head. "He is a good-looking kid. Smart, too. Really smart."

Baby bro is silent for a few seconds. "Anyway, he said that you're practically a shoo-win to get sole custody."

"Sole custody?"

"Yeah. She kept him away from you for this long. She lied to you. That speaks to her character."

He's right...again. I can definitely see how, in a court of law, they may look at Penelope's keeping Max a secret from me in a very negative light. Plus, the Warrens have connections and opportunities for Max that she can't even fathom.

"What would I need to do to get sole custody?" Even asking the question has my gut tightening, but I need all the information.

"He said he'll file the paperwork, and he'll take care of everything. Anything we can use against her to prove she's an unfit parent?"

"Prove she's unfit?"

I hadn't even thought about going that far. From what I can see, she's a wonderful mother and has done a great job with Max on her own. I can't take that away from him just because I'm angry about what she did.

Can I?

A door closes behind me, and I glance over my shoulder, but no one's there.

"Artie? You still there?"

I scrub a hand over my face. "Yeah, sorry. Look, I don't know what I'm going to do yet. You haven't said anything to anyone else, have you?"

He scoffs. "Of course not. I told Marcus this is strictly confidential. You know he won't say anything to Dad. Those two are like oil and water."

Thankfully, that's accurate. And it does give me a modicum of comfort to know that he's not going to run straight to Father to reveal my dirty little secret. It gives me a little bit more time to think. Although, with the storm letting up, I'm going to have to make a decision fast.

Archie sighs. "Look, Artemis, I know you used to love this girl. I remember how you walked around that summer with your head in the damn clouds. I haven't seen you like that since. But you can't let old feelings distract you from what happened here. She's been lying to you. She kept your son from you. You can offer him things a single mother never could. He could go to the best schools here in New York. He can have access to the best tutors. The best afterschool activities. The best of everything."

I clench my jaw. "He'll also have to deal with the rest of the Warrens."

"There are drawbacks to everything. You have to think big picture here. When it comes down to it, he's your son. Your flesh and blood. You deserve to have him, and you need to take him."

I end the call and shove my hand through my hair.

Could I do something like that to Penelope? Would she even try to keep him from me now, after everything that has happened?

Archie makes it seem so simple. So cut and dried.

That couldn't be further from the truth.

PENELOPE

I press my back to the wall in the bathroom and try to stop the world from spinning around me.

Sole custody.

Unfit mother.

I still can't believe I heard those words come out of Artemis' mouth.

He's going to take him. Even after everything that happened between us. After I gave myself to him. He's still going to take Max. And there's nothing I can do about it.

How can I fight with one of the most powerful families in the country? How can I compete with their high-priced lawyers and private investigators sent to uncover every dirty little secret I have?

Not that I have any.

Because of Max, my life has been very vanilla, very uneventful. But I know the Warrens, and they'll do whatever it takes to get what they want. And what Artemis wants is Max.

I should've known not to trust him. He is a Warren, after all, and he's had years under their thumb, toeing the Warren line. I should've known not to let him work his way under my skin again. I should've known that things weren't what they appeared and that I would end up getting hurt in the end.

Only it's not just going to be me. Max is the one who's going to pay for my mistake.

It doesn't matter that he and Artemis seem to get along so well; he's still going to be ripped from me, from Mom and Dad, from all of his friends and the whole life he's known with me.

He's going to be thrust into a life of rich assholes who don't care about anything unless it can get them ahead. He's going to be thrown into schools with kids who look down on him because of who he is and where he came from.

This is going to ruin his life and mine.

And it's all my fault.

I bite back a sob and try to gather my wits.

A lawyer. I need a lawyer.

I glance at my phone.

Shit.

It's three-fifteen in the morning.

Who's going to be up?

I call the only person I can think of.

Kristy answers the phone groggily. "Pen? Oh, my God. Do you have any idea what time it is? What's going on?"

"So much has happened since we talked last. I need your help."

"What happened?"

I suck in a huge breath, and then the words tumble from my mouth like word vomit. "I fucked up huge. I really thought we could be cordial. I thought we could make this thing work."

"What thing?"

"Max, the custody thing."

"Oh, no. What did you do?"

Something very, very stupid. "I let down my guard. I can't help it; he…he…Warrened me."

"He what?"

I shove away from the wall to look at myself in the mirror.

Jesus, was it only hours ago when I was in here having just seen him? Was it only hours ago when my world was turned upside down?

It feels more like years have passed during our confinement here.

"He Warrened me, Kristy. He has this…charm. He makes it so damn easy to love him."

"Jesus, Pen. Do you still have feelings for this guy?"

Kristy went through the post-Artemis ringer with me. She held my hand through the pregnancy and birth, and she's an aunt to Max, but I never told her I still held a candle for him, that deep down in my heart, I wanted him back. I knew she couldn't understand. Not really. You can't unless you've felt the love of that man.

"I do. I mean…I did. But after what I just heard…"

He just moved to the very bottom of my "people I like" list.

Kristy jostles the phone, probably dragging her ass out of bed. "What did you just hear?"

I don't even want to repeat the words. Each syllable feels like fire being ripped from my throat. "He was on the phone with somebody. He's going to try to take Max. He's going to try to prove I'm an unfit mother and go for sole custody."

"Jesus, Pen. I'm so sorry."

"It's not your fault." I shrug and stare at my reflection—a woman I barely recognize. So professional-looking. So adult. Yet so damn weak. "It's mine. For ever believing I could trust a Warren."

"So, what are you going to do?"

"I need a lawyer. A good one. And I need to talk to them fast."

Before the storm stops, they clear the runways, and Artemis is ready to fly out of here.

"Pen! It's three-thirty in the morning."

"I know. But I need to find somebody. You know anyone?"

Her work at the clerk of courts office should have exposed her to a lot of good lawyers. Hopefully, she has a decent relationship with some of them and can get one of them on the phone with me.

"Yeah, I know a lot of the lawyers. But they're all probably sound asleep in their beds because it's fucking Christmas, and it's three in the morning."

Shit. Shit. Shit.

"Pen, even if I called their offices, nobody's going to return phone calls on Christmas."

"What do I do, Kristy?"

Acid rises up my throat. I swallow it down. I'm not going to get sick. I'm going to hold it together.

She sighs. "I think all you can do right now is try to play nice and hope that he changes his mind."

I scoff and shove away from the sink. "If he were going to change his mind, he would've done that after we fucked."

"Holy shit, Penelope. You fucked him at the airport? With Max and your mom there?"

"Not my finest hour, trust me."

"I didn't realize it was this dire. I'll make some calls for you, but Pen, I'm telling you right now, don't get your hopes up. You might just have to deal with this after the holiday."

"What if he tries to take him when the runway is clear?"

"I don't know, sweetie. I don't know."

CHAPTER 15

ARTEMIS

That call rattled me. Actually, *rattled* would be an understatement.

Archimedes' suggestion—to go after sole custody, to try to prove she's an unfit mother—seems too cold and unfeeling. It's so...Warren. Everything I hate about them. But maybe he just sees the situation in a way I can't. He's a neutral party. He has no horse in this race.

Maybe I need to give what he recommended some serious consideration.

I run my fingers through my hair and tuck my phone back into my pocket. An unease has settled over me. An uncertainty. While Pen and I haven't talked about what will happen when the runway gets cleared, what happened between us in that back hallway had given me an apparently false sense of security with the situation. In reality, we've decided absolutely nothing.

If Clarence came to us right now and said we could take

off, we'd be left standing and staring at each other with no plan.

We need a plan.

I need to talk to Penelope.

As much as I'd love to go on pretending there isn't a giant five-year-old elephant in the room, we need to deal with the fact that someone may not walk away today happy.

Jolynn and Max sit together on the blanket, where we had our makeshift Christmas dinner.

Where the hell is Penelope?

I scan the small room, but there's no sign of her. Maybe she went to the office to check on the weather situation.

Max lays on his side, eating a granola bar, playing with his game. I settle in next to him, and he's none the wiser that his father sits a few inches away.

How are we ever going to explain this to him?

Kids can be so damn smart. So observant. Though I haven't spent a lot of time with rug rats, their uncanny ability to recognize certain aspects of human emotions and inter-play has always struck me as far too wise for their years.

Yet, Max hasn't seemed to figure out anything strange is going on with his mother and me. Perhaps it's only a matter of time.

"Mister Artie," he looks up at me from his resting spot, "you got any more of those chocolates? They'd be good with this Christmas feast."

This kid.

Before I can respond, Penelope appears standing over us. "I think you've had enough sugary processed foods to last you a lifetime, buddy."

Max's signature pout returns. "Aww, man, but they were really good, Momma."

"I bet they were."

I peer up at her from my seated position, giving her my best flirty smile. Despite all the internal turmoil tearing me apart right now, I can't seem to stop thinking about what just happened between us.

God, it was amazing to hold her, touch her, to be with her that way again.

Instead of a returned smile, Penelope stares back at me with icy coolness in her eyes. The harsh set of her jaw and stick-straight spine radiate anger.

What the hell happened?

Maybe she's upset Max hasn't had any real food since we've been here and is hopped up on a bunch of sugary crap. If this kid ingests much more junk food, we'll have to tie him to a chair to keep him still.

That's partially my fault with the chocolates, but I was just trying to do something nice for the kid...back before I even knew who he was. You'd think she'd see that instead of being pissed about it.

Penelope averts her eyes from my gaze and sits down beside her mother. Jolynn has remained surprisingly quiet, though I'm sure she observed Pen's cool response.

Try not to take it personally, Artemis.

Maybe she's just trying to keep her distance, so she doesn't confuse Max.

Even though I didn't know we were at war, I extend my arm with a peace offering. "Pen, would you like a granola bar?"

She scoffs and turns her head away from me. "I don't need anything from you. Never have."

What?

With her head turned away, the last few words were a little muffled and muted, but I'm pretty damn sure I heard her correctly.

What in the fuck is going on?

We just screwed each other's brains out like we were back to being those two hopeful and clueless teenagers, and now, she's acting like I'm a piece of shit on the bottom of her shoe.

When did that U-turn happen? And why?

It doesn't make sense. Unless she's just having a hard time trying to process everything that's happened in the last few hours. I mean, it has been pretty fucking overwhelming. She may be pondering the very same thing I just was—what's going to happen when that runway clears…

"Um, okay." I don't know how to respond to her, and I don't want to upset her any further. We both need to be in a good state of mind to have the inevitable conversation, if we don't want it to turn into an argument.

We've argued enough for a lifetime already.

So, instead of calling her out on her attitude, I turn my attention to Max. "If you could go camping anywhere, anywhere in the world, where would you go?"

Wherever it is. I'll make sure it happens.

He purses his lips and considers my question. He's the cutest damn kid.

Maybe I'm biased? Nah, he's adorable.

Penelope leans back, a sour expression still tarnishing her beautiful face.

What in the hell happened in that bathroom?

"I'd like to camp in my backyard, Mister Artie. I think it'd be the most fun ever. I'd have Momma, Grandma, Grandpa, and Mrs. Hensley, my teacher, and you, Mister Artie, all come over and camp with me. "

He included me.

It was a list of his favorite people.

My heart might explode.

Penelope shakes her head and scowls. "Mister Artie can't

come over and camp, honey. He's too busy, and he lives all the way in New York."

Is she trying to sabotage me now? What the hell is going on?

I glare at her and wrap my arm around Max. "I'd come visit you anytime, Max, and you can always come see me in New York."

I barely get the words out of my mouth before Penelope flies to her feet. "Artie, can I speak with you a moment? Alone."

She strides across the terminal toward the wall of windows overlooking the snow-covered tarmac. The wind outside has whipped snow drifts up against the building and everything else outside. It looks so bitter, so cold. Almost as bitter and cold as Penelope's attitude at this moment.

I follow in her wake, and confusion and just a bit of anger wrap themselves around me. I'm not quite sure what's going on, but her attitude speaks volumes at this moment. She's pissed.

Supremely pissed.

The only other time I've seen her this angry was the night she stormed away from me on that beach.

I don't understand. It seemed like things were fine—*more* than fine. This doesn't make any sense. Unless...she's having doubts about us, what happened between us moments ago.

God, maybe she regrets it. What if she feels like I took advantage of her?

Shit, did I? Take advantage of her? Of the situation? Did I misread things so badly?

She stands ramrod straight, staring blankly out the window, watching the snowflakes fly.

Why do I have the feeling things are about to implode?

"I'm not sure what's got you so upset, Penelope, but whatever it is, whatever I've done, I'm sorry. Talk to me. Let's fix this."

She closes her eyes as she slightly shakes her head. Finally, she seems to gather her thoughts enough to turn and face me. "How do you think this is going to work, Artie? How do you think you being in Max's life will actually work?"

Seriously? How can I possibly know the specifics yet? We haven't even talked about it.

I just found that he existed a few hours ago. She can't expect me to have a fully formulated plan already.

I sigh and rub my hand over my jaw. "I don't know. We'll just need to figure things out as we go."

"It doesn't work that way, Art. He's in school now. He has to go to school. And everything he's ever known is with me. We can't just 'wing it.' He can't fit into your schedule. You have to be willing to fit into his."

"I can do that. I'll do what I need to, but Pen…"

She talks right over me, as if I'm not here, and she can't bear to look at me. "This is why I didn't want to tell you. The Warrens are your priority. He won't be."

I growl low and take a step toward her. "He would have been my priority had I known. And I'm making him one now. You two will move to New York so I can make up for all the time with him you stole from me. I fucking deserve that."

Her gaze narrows on me, and fire dances across her cool green eyes.

Shit. I said the completely wrong thing.

She clenches her teeth and fists her hand at her sides. "You would think that, wouldn't you? Everyone should give up everything and move because it's easier for you."

Yeah, shit. Definitely the wrong thing to say.

138

PENELOPE

The nerve of this man...

He's absolutely infuriating.

It shouldn't surprise me, though. He's had years of being the impeccable Warren son. Plenty of time to perfect becoming the self-centered jerk he obviously is. Of course, he thinks everyone should just drop everything and do as he commands.

It's the Warren way.

I honestly don't know why I thought things could work between us, how they could be any different.

Before, we were children. We were young and hopeful and naïve, dreaming of things we had no damn clue about. He wasn't a Warren robot back then. But the last six years have changed him. He doesn't just look like his father; he's become him.

I knew it would happen. He will never be able to leave that part of his life behind. The job, the name, the empire. I suspected it then, and now—coupled with that phone call he just had—he's just proven it to me.

He only wants what's best for him.

"I mean I...," he stammers, now choosing his words more carefully. "Shit, I'm sorry. I just assumed it would be easiest for all of us. There are so many jobs available in New York. You could easily find one. There are great schools for Max to attend. It just seems like the best idea."

He rubs the back of his neck.

He's stressed. Good.

Of course, I knew his finding out the truth would mean big changes for Max and me. I can't keep Artemis away from his son any longer. But I had imagined some sort of custody agreement. Maybe he could spend summers and holidays with Artemis and the school year with me. That seems reasonable, given the circumstances. Given that his entire life, all his friends and everything he knows are with me. He barely knows Artemis. Anything more would be…insanity.

How dare he even consider taking my son from me.

I haven't been able to shake the words "sole custody" and "unfit mother" from my ears. He's willing to throw me under the bus to take Max, yet he's standing here, pretending he wants to work something out. He acts as if uprooting our lives and dragging us to New York isn't a big deal. And maybe it's not compared to taking him from me completely, but it's still delusional to believe I would ever let either of those things happen.

He doesn't know a thing about children, about having a family. I guess I've played a part in that, and for that, I'll always carry a heavy weight of regret, but right now, he needs to get his head out of his ass.

Shit. Shit. Shit.

But, until I talk to an attorney, I can't let him know I overheard his call. I'm not sure what he would do with that information. How he would use it against me. Right now, I have the upper hand. I know what he's really planning and can see through the façade he's putting up.

I just need to play along until I can get some advice on how to proceed, which will hopefully come soon because the storm is letting up. It won't be too long before we'll be flying out of here.

Until then, I just need to stay strong.

Don't fall into the Warren trap again, Pen.

I would love to trust him. I want to believe there's some misunderstanding here, but there isn't. I heard what I heard. And that was enough for me to close my heart again to Artemis Warren.

It's the only way to protect myself *and* Max.

"Taking Max from his life isn't 'the best idea,' Artemis. It's going to be hard enough for him to adjust to being told you're his father without also ripping away all the people and places he knows and loves. New York isn't any place to raise a child. Look what it did to you."

He recoils slightly.

Shit. Maybe that was a bit too harsh.

But part of me wanted to wound him with my words. The same way what he said on the phone drove a knife straight into my heart.

His eyes darken with his pain, and the old need to comfort him tries to hack its way out of my chest. But Artemis Warren doesn't need saving. He's perfectly capable of taking care of himself. He's more than proven that over the hours we've spent here together.

He shoves a hand through his hair and sighs. "If that's what you think of me, Pen, then I must have completely misread what's happened here tonight."

No.

He didn't misread it at all. I fell hook, line, and sinker for the Artemis Warren I thought he still was. The one he was all those years ago. But that's not who the man standing in front of me is anymore. That Artemis would never...*could* never try to take my child from me, no matter what the circumstances were, no matter *how* angry or hurt he might be by what I had done.

I let myself be swept away in old feelings and desires I tried to push down and ignore for so long. I let myself be my focus instead of Max for just a few moments, and it was long enough for Artemis to work his way into my heart again.

It's *my* fault. Not his. He doesn't even realize when he's doing it. It's just a natural Warren attribute. Engrained in their DNA. They're manipulators. Through and through.

I clear my throat of the lump sitting there and shake my head. "I'm sorry, Artemis, but whatever it is you think was happening was in your head. I scratched an itch with an old flame. Forced proximity makes people do strange things. Nothing more."

The words burn—both Artemis and me.

It's like watching him be struck by a hail of bullets from a firing squad. But I can't feel sorry for him. Not after what I heard. Not after what he said.

Stand your ground, Pen. Don't give in.

CHAPTER 16

ARTEMIS

I've never seen Pen like this. Even when we ended things, when she thought the worst of me, she wasn't like this. She's being...spiteful. Almost like she wants to hurt me. That's so not her. That's not the Penelope I know and love.

Two steps close the distance between us, and I grab her biceps and force her to look at me. "Tell me what's really going on, Pen. This isn't you."

Her shimmering, tear-soaked eyes stare back at me for a moment, and her mouth opens, ready to argue. Then she swallows. "I wasn't going to tell you. Not until I knew what my rights were, but there's no sense in playing games with a Warren. Not when you always win."

What the hell is she talking about?

"I'm not playing any games, Penelope."

One of her dark brows rises. "I heard you, Artemis. On your phone call. You're going to sue me for sole custody and try to prove I'm an unfit mother. You're going to take him from me."

Shit.

"No, Penelope. You misunderstood—"

"Did I?" She tugs out of my grip and takes a step back. "Who were you talking to? Your father? One of your family lawyer friends? A judge you have in your back pocket?"

God. No wonder she's so fucking pissed.

If I had overheard my side of that conversation, it's exactly what I would think too.

I shake my head. "No. The only person who knows is Archimedes."

She snorts and tosses her head back to stare at the ceiling for a moment. "Of course. Your little brother. He's just another weapon in the Warren arsenal, isn't he?"

Yeah, kind of.

"It isn't like that, Pen. I told him because I needed to talk out the situation with someone I knew I could trust. Someone who *wouldn't* tell my parents or grandparents."

"So, the entire conversation was innocent? I didn't hear what I think I heard?"

Crap.

She's got me there. It really wasn't innocent. Not at all.

"I just needed to talk to a friend, Pen. Someone who was on *my* side in all this. A neutral party who wouldn't let his personal feelings about you fog his logic."

She frowns and takes another step back. "That's what I do? Fog your logic?"

"Christ, Pen. I haven't had a single cognizant thought around you since the moment I laid eyes on you that summer. You completely unravel me."

Even only a few hours ago, those words probably would have been viewed by her as some sort of major declaration. A sign that my feelings are real. But now, she stares at me with confusion and anger rolling off her in waves.

She crosses her arms over her chest as if they offer her

some protection from me. "How does that all lead to you taking Max from me?"

"Oh, come on, Pen. You had to know I needed to find out all of my options. It would be stupid not to. Archimedes suggested those two things. They had never even crossed my mind until then."

She bites her bottom lip and rolls her eyes. "Sure, you hadn't." Her gaze darts across the terminal to where Max and Jolynn are still gloriously unaware of the argument happening over here. "Look, Artie, maybe we should just leave this to our attorneys. I think that may be what's best for everyone involved."

Leave it to our attorneys? Is she fucking serious?

I have to take a second before I can respond to her. The words won't form in my head to express how totally twisted I am. "How did it come to this, Pen? How did we go from," I lean into her to ensure no prying ears will hear me, "from fucking in a dark corner to not even being able to have a discussion as adults without going through intermediaries?"

"It came to this when you even *considered* taking Max from me. I know I have to pay the price for what I did in keeping him from you, but I don't deserve *that*. I don't deserve to lose him."

I reach up and cup her cheek, a gesture she's leaned into so many times.

Not now.

She pulls away.

I drop my hand. "You don't deserve that, Pen. And I never would have done that. I swear."

"Unfortunately, I learned a long time ago not to believe a Warren."

That stings more than she can possibly know. She has no idea how much I agree with her on that. On how much I know it to be true. I just never thought she'd group me in with them that way. I thought she understood how I felt about the family back then and how I still feel.

There are a lot of things about each other we've failed to see. Whether we've been blinded by old feelings, lust, or misplaced love for Max, it seems we've both paid the price while trapped here in this airport.

One I'm sure we'll both feel for a very long time.

"Miss Barnes? Mister Warren?"

We both turn toward Clarence. He stands a few feet away from us, his bushy, white brows raised in concern. "Sorry to interrupt. I thought you two would want to know that the storm is letting up. It should only be a few hours at most before we can get the runway cleared enough for your planes to take off."

Perfect fucking timing.

PENELOPE

I use the distraction of Clarence's arrival to slip away from Artemis and back over to Mom and Max. The moment Artemis started talking to him, I bolted across the terminal.

Being anywhere near Artemis sucks me into his orbit. Into a place where I can't control myself. His explanation was *this close* to bringing me to believe him. I was right there, dangling on the precipice of throwing myself into his arms and begging him to come with us to figure out a way to make things work.

I'm so damn weak.

Even now, I glance over my shoulder at where he stands, talking to Clarence, undoubtedly asking piloty questions I wouldn't understand.

Mom and Max glance up at me. She gives me a knowing

look. There's no way she missed that fight. We may have managed to keep our voices down for Max's sake, but the body language should have said everything she needed to know to assess the situation.

She plasters on a smile. "What did Clarence say?"

I settle on the other side of Max. "Good news. The storm is almost over. We should be out of here in a few hours, tops."

Max twists to look at me. "What about Mister Artie?"

My chest tightens. I should have seen that question coming and prepared myself. "What do you mean, buddy?"

He chews on his bottom lip. "Is he coming with us?"

The knife in my heart twists, just a little deeper. "No, buddy. Mister Artie lives in New York. He needs to go home."

There's no need to try to explain the truth right now, not when things are so undecided. He will have too many questions that I won't have answers to yet. Ones that could really hurt him...and me.

"But...when are we going to see him again?"

It's possible no human being has ever been torn into two directions at once so hard before. Part of me wants to say never. The other part knows Artie will be a fabulous father, and continuing to try to keep Max from him would be the most selfish thing I've ever done.

There's only one answer I know for sure is the truth. "You'll see him again, buddy. I just don't know when yet."

He pouts and jumps to his feet to rush over to the chairs along the wall again. Mom starts to rise to go after him.

"No." I hold out a hand. "Let him be by himself for a couple minutes. He's not going anywhere. And we need to talk. Alone."

She nods. "I thought we might need to. What happened? Your whole attitude toward Artemis seemed to flip in the last hour."

I bury my face in my hands. "God, Mom. Things have gone to shit so fast. I don't even know how to wrap my head around it."

Her warm hand lands on my shoulder, and she gives it a gentle squeeze. "Tell me what happened."

"Artemis talked to his brother. I overheard him say he was going to try for sole custody and to prove I'm an unfit mother."

"What?" Mom recoils.

I glance over my shoulder at her. "Yeah. I called Kristy and asked her to find me a good family lawyer, but it's Christmas. I don't know that she'll be able to get a hold of anyone before we're ready to leave."

"You don't think Artemis would try to take him when he leaves today, do you?"

A few hours ago, when Artemis had me pressed against that wall, when he was moving inside me and kissing me senseless, I would have said no without even considering it. But now...

"I have no idea, Mom. I sure as hell hope not."

But I have *no idea* what the legalities of this are.

If he walks away with Max, takes off on that plane of his and flies back to New York, would he really be in trouble?

There's nothing legal proving he's Max's father, no DNA test, no birth certificate. But that doesn't mean the law would do anything about it.

These are the Warrens. His grandfather was a Supreme Court Justice for fuck's sake. You can't *get* any more connected than that.

What district attorney is going to file charges against Artemis Warren the III for kidnapping his own son once a DNA test comes back?

None. That's who.

So, what power do I really have here?

None.

Clarence walks past us on his way back to the office. I peek over at Artemis, hoping to somehow be able to glean where he stands on this whole thing, but all I find is his back to me, his phone against his ear again.

Whoever he's talking to...it can't be good.

I doubt he's calling Archimedes to tell him how insane his suggestions were. And he sure isn't coming over here to assure me he won't touch Max.

This day went from the worst to the best, and back to the worst again so fast, I have whiplash.

Mom grabs my shoulder and tugs. "Pen."

"What?"

She holds my phone up in front of my face. "Your phone is ringing."

Unknown number.

Normally, I wouldn't answer it, but right now, I'm desperate for a lifeline.

CHAPTER 17

PENELOPE

"You're choosing a big enemy, Miss Barnes. The Warrens don't like to be challenged, especially where their family is concerned. You've kept an heir a secret from them. That won't be taken lightly."

Like he's telling me anything I don't already know.

Saying the Warrens are a big enemy is like saying Jaws was a large shark.

Mike Hall is a great lawyer—according to the text I got from Kristy almost as soon as my phone rang. He seems to really know his shit. It hasn't helped ease any of my fears, though.

"But does that give Artemis a legal leg to stand on? Does it give him a basis to take Max from me?"

That's the question I've been waiting to have answered. I've already explained to Attorney Hall that the runway will be cleared soon, and even if Artie doesn't try to take him today, he will come for him eventually. Warrens aren't known for their patience. It won't surprise me if he shows up on Mom and Dad's doorstep tomorrow with a court order.

Mister Hall sighs. "You could contact the local police there. Explain the situation. Tell them there's no legal finding as to paternity and no custody agreement permitting Mister Warren to take Maxwell with him. But…"

There's always a but…

"That could get ugly. And in front of your son. If you want him to have a good relationship with his father, and *you* want to maintain any semblance of a cordial relationship with his father, then I highly suggest you make another attempt to talk to Mister Warren before that tarmac is cleared."

I was afraid he'd say that. I don't know if I have the strength to go another round with that man.

My silence must give away my reluctance.

"Miss Barnes, I understand how extremely trying this situation is for all involved. I've dealt with some very contentious custody battles in my career. And one thing I've learned in three decades in the courtroom is that the children who always end up winning are the ones whose parents don't consider them a prize or a weapon to use against one another."

"That's not what I'm doing."

"Let me finish, Miss Barnes. You may not be doing that, but my point, if you had let me continue, is that those parents who work together to do what's in the best interest of the child, the ones who put their *own* feelings aside, those are the ones whose children are happiest."

It's exactly why I kept hoping things could work out amicably between us, but Artemis is making that impossible by tugging at my heartstrings and throwing my greatest fear at me.

"Could he prove I'm an unfit mother and get sole custody if that's what he really wants?"

"He can *try* to do whatever he wants, Miss Barnes. And knowing the Warrens, they won't even hesitate to stoop to less than legal or ethical levels to achieve their goal. From what you and your friend have told me, there's nothing in your past that points to any concern for how you care for Maxwell. In fact, I think most courts would agree, you've done a wonderful job on your own, and you provide a stable, happy living environment for him."

That eases a bit of the tension in my shoulders. If a lawyer thinks that, then I'm not a totally shitty parent.

"But you cannot discount the Warren name."

And there it is.

That name has been the bane of my existence for so long…hearing someone else confirm how powerful and unscrupulous they are actually feels like more of a win than it should. It certainly isn't good news.

"The opportunities it will present to Maxwell if he were to live with Artemis, and the fact that Artemis was denied the ability to raise his child will come into play. The court will always do what's in the best interests of the child, and there is a very real chance, that could be split custody or even sole custody to him after a period of adjustment for Maxwell. If we ended up in front of a judge who was swayed by the Warrens in some fashion—whether through promises or threats—that outcome could be even more devastating for you."

I sigh and recline back in the hard-plastic chair down just a few from Mom and Max. "So, my only hope is to reason with him and come to an agreement. That's what you're saying?"

"Pretty much, Miss Barnes. Believe me, I know it's not what you want to hear right now. And I do feel for you…this all happening on Christmas and like this. It really seems some twist of fate has happened."

No shit.

It doesn't sound like I have much choice. I have to do what's best for Max. And the attorney is right, that isn't having the police show up to intervene with Artemis. Max already loves the man, even without knowing who he truly is. I see it in the way Max is with Artemis every moment they've spent together. He's desperately searching for a father figure without even realizing he's doing it, and now his real father is sitting right here, begging to be part of his life.

Surely, we can work something out that doesn't involve firearms and badges.

"I'll talk to him again."

"Excellent. Please, keep me posted, Miss Barnes. Now, if you'll excuse me, I am going to try to get a few more hours of sleep before my grandkids arrive at the crack of dawn to open their gifts."

"Thank you again for taking the time to speak with me, today of all days."

"You're very welcome, Miss Barnes."

The line goes dead.

It's time to summon up every ounce of courage I have to try to get this resolved.

ARTEMIS

"You're a dad. Wow. I mean, what the fuck, Artie?" Athena chuckles. "Honestly, I figured, if anybody would have a baby, out of the three of us, my money was on Archie. He can't seem to keep it in his pants."

In spite of the way I feel right now, a little laugh bubbles up. "Yeah, I'm a dad. It's crazy."

Beyond crazy.

Today has been, without a doubt, the most emotionally exhausting day of my life.

But there's one amazing thing that has come from all the pain and turmoil.

"He's amazing, Athena. I can't wait for you to meet him."

Whenever that is.

And therein lies the problem. I have no idea when I'll see Max again or under what circumstances. With the contentious way things just went down with Penelope, for the first time today, I'm starting to question whether she'll try to keep him from me.

Athena yawns. It's barely dawn, and I woke her up after a late night of drinking to deal with the pretentious lot at the party. "He's part of you. I'm sure he's amazing. But did you call just to tell me about Max? Couldn't that have waited until…I don't know…the sun comes up?"

"Shit. I'm sorry, Athena. But…his mom," I rub the back of my neck, "I just can't seem to say the right things, do the right things where she's concerned. And it's affecting what's going to happen with Max."

Maybe she wasn't wrong to keep him hidden from me. I damn sure don't seem to know what to do to fix any of this. Despite my best intentions, I'm failing them in an epic way.

I've let this situation bring out the worst in me. After the argument we just had, I actually considered Archimedes' suggestion to strip Penelope of custody. I actually considered trying to dig up dirt on her.

As if there is any.

Penelope is a wonderful person. She doesn't deserve any of this, no matter how badly she wounded me by keeping Max a secret.

"Athena," I stare out at the white, glittery wonderland outside. A few stray flakes continue to fall, but the brunt of the storm has dissipated, creating a sparkling landscape that would be damn stunning if I were in any mindset to appreciate it. "I didn't mean for her to think for one moment I would take Max away. I would never do that. I could never do that to her."

To him.

"I know, Art. You don't have that in you. It's not me you need to convince of that fact. At some point, you're going to have to talk to her. You have to make her understand where you're coming from. You left things up in the air the last time you saw this woman, and look at how that turned out—with a kid you never knew existed."

A tractor pulls out onto the tarmac and starts pushing through the snow, creating massive piles along the side of the runway. I have to fix this. We'll be able to leave soon. Pen and Max and I will fly off in different directions, and I can't leave things the way they are.

"You're right. I know you're right. I'm just not sure she'll even speak to me now."

I glance over to where Penelope sits, talking on her phone. Even with her head dropped down, the stress on her face, the worry, and fear there might as well be stamped out in words. I can't blame her for going all "Momma bear" on me. Max has been her world for five years. This is a lot for her to deal with in one day. A lot for *anyone* to deal with.

"Shit. How do I fix this mess?"

"You tell her the truth, Artie. You keep telling her the truth until she listens. Even as a kid, I could see how much you loved her, how much she meant to you. And I assume some of those feelings are still there."

All of those feelings are still there, and then some. I will never love anyone the way I love Penelope Barnes. Period.

"Thanks, sis. When did you become the most logical of the Warrens?"

Her laugh shoots through the line, and I can't help but smile. Though she may march to her own beat, Athena will always be the most levelheaded of us. It's probably why she's such a black sheep. Mom and Dad don't want anyone analyzing anything with logic. They like the kind of sheep who blindly follow to the slaughter.

"Someone has to be. All the rest of you are a big fucking mess."

No shit.

"Thank you for listening, Athena. And thanks for the advice."

"Anytime, Art. Now, go fix things with your baby momma. I love you."

The line goes dead. I return my phone to my pocket.

How can I implement what Athena said? How can I get Pen to listen to me when every time we try to speak, things get twisted and misunderstood?

I need to formulate a plan. Then, I can talk to Penelope. But it looks like I won't have time to do that. Penelope is heading straight toward me.

Shit.

Her long, toned legs bring her closer, and despite our current predicament, I can't help but recall how fantastic it was to have them wrapped around me back in that hallway.

Before everything turned to shit.

I shake the vision from my mind. I need to stop thinking about that, or I won't have a clear head while having this conversation. As enjoyable as reliving every moment of being with her is, this isn't the time or the place.

She straightens her shoulders and sucks in a deep breath. "Artie, can I talk to you?" One of her hands shoots up to stop me from responding. "Talk. Not argue. Just talk?"

That would be a refreshing change.

And a much-needed one.

"Of course, Penelope." I motion toward her with my hand, signaling her to start the conversation we so desperately need to have.

She obviously has something she needs to say.

I do, too, but after what happened last time we spoke, I think it's best if I keep my mouth shut long enough to hear her out first.

She takes a deep breath and closes her eyes like she's trying to center herself and find some elusive calm. "I'm sorry. I'm sorry for going off on you like I did. Fear was overriding my senses. You have every right to explore every avenue where your son is concerned."

Wait...what?

She's sorry?

It's the last thing I thought she'd say.

I clear my throat, nerves choking my words. Fear steals my ability to speak. If I say the wrong thing, it could send us back down that angry, shitty path we traveled earlier. "I never meant for you to think I would take Max away from you. I wouldn't do that. I could never do that to you or to him. I will always do what's best for him..." This part is going to sting because I never thought I'd say these words. "And if that means leaving New York and moving to be near you and Max, that's what I'll do. I don't want to disrupt his life. I just want to be a part of it."

Her eyes widen, and then, she closes them again and shakes her head before reopening them. "I'd like to say I believe you, but I'm sorry. I can't. Too much of our history proves to me that's not true. You can't leave your family. Your life. You won't."

That hurt.

She doesn't think me capable of taking a selfless action

like that. Everything that's gone down has blinded her to who I really am—still just that boy she fell in love with on that beach.

"Penelope, what if I told you I was on my way to New York City, to the family holiday party, where I intended to announce I was leaving Warren Enterprises?"

Her mouth falls open, but no sound comes out. It's exactly the reaction I had expected at the party.

"Those were my plans yesterday, before this storm brought me to you and to Max. I wanted to make the announcement somewhere public. Somewhere Father and Grandfather couldn't cause a scene. I've wanted out for a while, but now, I have even more incentive to leave. I will walk away, Penelope. I will. This," I motion between us, "gives me even more reason to do so."

I can't work for Father anymore. I can't keep destroying lives just to bulk up the family coffers. It felt shitty and wrong before. Even more so now that I have a son I need to set an example for. Father and Grandfather have let greed—for money and power—cloud their judgment and direct their actions for far too long. I will be better than them.

It may have taken me a long time to break free from the Warren chains, but I'm doing it.

I take the few steps separating us and pull her arms in my hands. "I love you, Pen. I have always loved you. For me, you're it. And I already love Max. You've done such an amazing job with him, and I will do anything, anything to keep you in my life. Because Penelope, you and Max *are* my family."

Her green eyes shimmer before a tear trickles down her cheek. A war rages inside her—between believing what I just said and returning to her mistrust. "Seeing is believing, Artemis. And I haven't seen anything that suggests you're any different than your family. I'm sorry, but I just can't believe that. Your promises may be enough for Max, and of course, he would love if you moved to Nashville to be close to him, but they aren't for me. I can't give you my heart again. I'm sorry. I just can't."

And there it is.

No matter what I say or what I do, it seems I will never be able to reconcile my past and my present as far as Penelope is concerned.

She's been hurt too badly, by me, by misunderstandings, by life. The uncertainty she carries just can't be overcome, and that breaks my heart all over again.

CHAPTER 18

ARTEMIS

A massive plow moves past the row of windows. The runway is almost clear.

Finally, I can get out of this little slice of Hell on Earth. I don't think my heart can bear much more.

This has been the furthest thing from a Merry Christmas, besides learning about the existence of my son. It's been a twenty-four-hour rollercoaster. I'm beaten and battered from the emotional turmoil.

Nothing I say can convince Penelope of the truth. All she sees is a Warren. That's all she will ever see.

I don't want to give up. I did that once, and look where it got us. But the last several hours have put me through the wringer, and I'm just fucking tired. Tired of arguing, tired of trying to convince her of my feelings for her, just plain tired of my feelings, because no matter what I do, I still love Penelope Barnes.

Probably always will.

Knowing things will just never work out between us is

the ultimate blow to my heart. She doesn't trust me. She doesn't trust my family or their motives. And the worst part is, I can't blame her.

She spent years protecting herself and Max from being hurt, and in less than twenty-four hours, I've practically destroyed her.

Unintentionally, but it's true just the same.

Why do things have to end this way?

I'm not a bad man. In fact, I'm a good enough man to see that my actions are causing the woman I love harm, and I'm man enough to recognize I need to walk away.

No matter how much it hurts. No matter how much everything in my being is screaming at me to fight, I just can't let my love for Penelope destroy her anymore. So, I'll let her go. However, I will not walk away from my son.

I want to get to know Max. I want to be his dad. And for that, I will fight if I need to. But I'm hoping some time and space might give Penelope the room she needs to breathe and see things in a different light.

This back and forth isn't good for her or Max.

They are my priority now. I need to think about their well-being. And if walking away from the one woman I have ever loved, even if it breaks my heart, makes things even a little bit better, then that's what I'll do.

I turn back toward the terminal. Penelope and Jolynn help Max get all his little toys back into his bag.

Seeing that origami heart clutched in his tiny little hand breaks something inside me. I slap at the tears before they can fall. It's time to resign myself to the fact that Max's mother and father just can't be together, no matter how much I may want that.

After one last look at the family that could have been, I grab my things and approach Max to tell him goodbye. It won't be for long, though. Very soon, we're going to have a conversation about who I am, and a court will make a custody order. I won't play dirty, but I will ensure I get to see Max as much as possible.

"We're going to Grandpa's now?" Max's excited tone as he talks to Pen eases just a little bit of the pain I'm feeling.

He'll get to have a Christmas after all. Even if I can't be a part of it.

This year...

Because I damn sure don't intend to miss any other important days of Max's life.

Penelope's back is to me.

"I just wanted to say goodbye to Max."

Her body stiffens at the sound of my voice, and she turns to face me. I have to fight the urge to grab her, hug her, and shake some sense into her. Beg her to please, please just listen to what I have to say for once.

But I won't do that.

My heart just can't take much more rejection from Penelope Barnes.

"Go ahead, Artie." She motions between Max and me.

His sparkling blue eyes and adorable little smile bring one to my lips even though I feel like I'm shattering into a million pieces.

He has no idea his little life is about to change, hopefully for the better. He also has no idea his parents are broken-hearted.

I squat down in front of him so I'm on his level. "Hey, buddy. I'm really glad I got to meet you. And I have a feeling, I'll be seeing you again real soon. Okay?"

His little hand comes out to shake mine. "Okay, Mister Artie. I can't wait. You can come to my house. I have more games we can play."

My soul wrenches a little more. I have to walk off and leave the most important people in this world to me standing here, with no definitive plans of when I see them again.

"I'd love to, buddy. That sounds great."

Max's arms wrap around my neck, and he squeezes. I hug him back.

Shit. I never want to let him go again.

A sniffle draws my attention up. Penelope swipes a stray tear from her eye.

"You take good care of your mom for me, Max, okay?"

"I will, Mister Artie."

I pull back from Max and hold him at arm's length, taking one more look before I have to leave him. "I'll see you soon, buddy."

"Bye-bye, Mister Artie."

Jolynn takes Max's hand and walks him a few feet away to give Penelope and me a final moment together.

I won't leave without saying this. "I know you won't believe me, Pen, but I was going to that party so I could announce publicly, in front of my family, their fake friends, and their business associates that I was leaving the family business."

"It doesn't really matter now, does it? It didn't happen."

She doesn't believe me.

Why would she?

"Here." She slips a piece of paper into my hand. "It's all my contact information. Call me. We can work out something, some way for you to spend time with Max, that we both can agree on. Take care, Artie."

So cold. So formal. No opening to make things right.

I nod my agreement and wave to Jolynn. "Take care, ladies. Bye, Max."

It's the hardest thing I've ever done, walking away and leaving them…

Again.

I don't look back.

I can't.

If I do, I'll only fall at Penelope's feet and beg her to let me love her. I've pretty much done that, and it got me nowhere.

I push open the terminal doors. A blast of cold air shocks my system. It's welcome. I need something to keep me from turning back. But it can't keep me from taking one last look at Max and Penelope.

PENELOPE

Tears slip down my cheeks as the man I love walks away from me again.

God. I want so badly to believe him.

If he really had planned to fly to New York and leave Warren Enterprises, break away from the hold the Warrens have on him and be his own man, it would change everything.

But I just can't let myself believe that. He said it before, made similar promises, and look where we wound up. In less than twenty-four hours, Artemis has managed to break my heart all over again.

At least this time, something good will come of the pain. We've managed to make things better for Max. Having his father in his life will change everything for him.

Artemis reaches the door, and he looks back at Max and me before he walks out into the snow and out of my heart again. Forever, this time.

I slump down into the nearest chair and drop my head into my hands—my body too weak, too beaten down by all the emotions, for me to trust my ability to stand on my own two feet anymore.

"Honey, what the hell are you doing?"

Mom's question makes me drag my face from my hands. "Um, trying not to cry."

She stands in front of me, hands on her hips, and a scowl turning her lips down. "That's not what I'm talking about. Why are you letting the only man you've ever loved walk away? You've been down this road before, Penelope. You know what a life without Artemis in it looks like. Do you love him? Really? Do you really love him?"

Mom's tone catches me off guard. There's anger there mixed with the concern.

Why is she mad?

"Of course, I love him. I have been in love with him since the first moment I saw him. I just can't trust him. I can't trust his intentions. He makes promises he doesn't intend to keep."

"He has good tensions, Momma."

I jerk at Max's voice and look to where he's standing. I hadn't even realized he came over. I never meant to word vomit with him standing there. I just have no control over myself these last twenty-four hours, it seems. Seeing Artemis has turned everything upside down.

"What's that, baby?" I reach a hand toward Max.

He climbs up onto my lap. "Mister Artie said he only wants you to have more happiness than you can stand."

"Oh, how sweet." Mom smiles and swipes away an errant tear. "I've never cried more at an airport in my life."

Me, either.

And what Max just said has thrown me. "What do you mean, Max? He told you that?"

"I asked him, Momma. I asked him what his tensions are. Mister Artie says his tensions are good. Real good."

His intentions are good?

He told our son his intentions are good.

While I may not trust Artemis, I know, beyond a shadow

of the doubt, he would never lie to his son. He just doesn't have that in him.

Could he have been telling me the truth? Would he walk away from the Warrens?

I blink away my tears and look up at Mom.

Her eyebrows rise, and she points toward the door out to the runway. "If you don't go get him, I'm going to go get him. Get up, Penelope. Bring him back."

She lifts Max from my lap.

Bring him back.

The words click together slowly.

Bring him back.

I push to my feet.

Shit.

I let him go. I let him walk away this time. It's a mistake. A huge one.

One I made years ago that left wounds so deep, they allowed the lingering pain to taint what's happening now.

I have to bring him back.

If he leaves now, I may never be able to fix this.

My legs wobble.

Stupid heels.

Every step on the tiny stiletto is risking my ankles, but I run.

It's only been a few minutes since Artemis walked out that door.

But, oh, God. What if he's gone? What if I'm too late?

Our pilot steps from the office, and I almost plow right into him. "Miss Barnes? Is everything all right?"

"It will be! I have to stop Artemis!"

His hand snaps out, and he catches my arm. "You can't go out there like this." He waves his free hand up and down. "You'll freeze to death."

He's probably right. But I don't care.

Nothing matters except getting to Artemis.

I tug my arm free from the pilot's grasp and burst through the doors of the terminal out to the blistering cold.

Holy shit! It's fucking freezing.

And slippery.

My heels slide through the snow and across the icy pavement. The wind whips at my bare legs, this suit dress no match for these temperatures.

It doesn't matter. I can deal with a little cold. It's a fitting punishment for the way I treated Artemis. I froze him out. I pushed him away and refused to believe his sincerity. I caused this. And I need to fix it.

"Miss Barnes? What on Earth are you doing out here? It's freezing!" Clarence stands a few feet to my left.

I hadn't even noticed him there.

"Clarence! Thank God! Can you help me? Where is Artemis Warren?"

Please don't say he left already.

Clarence's brow furrows, and he glances behind him. "Go down to the end of this building and make a left. He's readying for take-off, but he hasn't left yet."

Thank God.

Another cold blast of wind gives my goose bumps goose bumps, and I rub my arms. "You're a lifesaver, Clarence. An angel among men. Merry Christmas!"

Though he still wears his confusion, he offers me a smile. "Merry Christmas, Miss Barnes."

The blustery wind whips his words and carries them off. I barely hear them before I take off toward the direction he pointed.

A plane engine fires up from somewhere around the corner of the large hangar.

Shit. I'm too late.

I push my legs harder, and my heel slips out from under

me. The ground rushes up at me. Icy snow stings my legs and arm, but I ignore it and climb to my feet again.

Only a few feet left before I can turn that corner and flag him down.

Don't go, Artemis. Please!

I rush around the corner, and my heart stops.

A small plane sits at the start of the runway—Artemis at the controls.

"No! Don't go! Artemis! Artemis, wait!" I wave and rush toward the plane.

Coming from the side, Artemis can't see me. He stares straight ahead, completely oblivious. And the sound of the engine combined with the still whipping wind swallow my plea.

"Stop! Artemis, stop!"

Tears roll down my cheeks.

He can't go. He can't leave without me telling him I love him.

I swing my arms frantically, desperate to get his attention. He glances toward me, then does a double-take.

The engine powers down. It's music to my weary soul. The small door to the cabin pops open, and Artemis peeks his head out.

His eyes narrow on me. "Pen, what's wrong?"

"Everything!" I shout back.

He hops out of the plane and rushes toward me, sheer panic in his steps.

I caught him.

He's still here.

And I don't care anymore. I don't care what's right. I don't care what's wrong. I love him. I love him with everything I am, everything I was, and everything I ever will be. It's all wrapped up in this man.

I leap into his arms.

He catches me and clutches me against his strong, warm body. "Pen?"

"I'm sorry. I'm sorry for everything, Artie. I'm just so sorry." I pull back so he can see my eyes. So he can *see* how desperate and sincere I am. "Please...please forgive me. Forgive me for what I've done. Forgive me for not believing in you. Forgive me for being so fucking stupid. I love you. And I can't let you go again. I can't bear it."

He squeezes me just a little bit tighter. His eyes search mine. "You love me?"

God, yes.

More than I ever thought possible.

"More than anything on this Earth. Well, besides our son."

A slow grin spreads across Artemis' lips, and he leans into me and presses his forehead against mine. "I'll happily play second fiddle to him."

Relief floods my system. A warm, sweeping glow that makes the cold of the air surrounding us almost non-existent.

I push my lips to his, kissing him with a passion that has been burned into my soul since I was a seventeen-year-old girl. One that has never dissipated. Never gone away.

Clutching to him like my life depends on it—because it does—I give him everything. I put it all into that kiss.

One kiss.

A statement.

I love you. I'm never letting you go again. You are my home.

EPILOGUE

SIX MONTHS LATER

PENELOPE

How is this my life?

    Ocean waves sweep gently up on the beach only a few yards away from the back porch of our house on Cape Harmony. Artie chases Max around in the sand, the water lapping at their bare feet. Max's excited squeal, followed by Art's joyful chuckle, warm my heart in a way I never thought possible.

"Daddy, you can't catch me!" Max's little taunt ends with Art scooping him up and raising him over his head in a fit of giggles.

Finally, my family is whole.

When we sat Max down on New Year's Day and explained to him that Artemis is his father, I never antici-pated how easily things would fall into place. Art had to leave for a while to get things settled with his family, but he promised Max he would be back and would never leave for long again.

Max took it better than we expected. His first question

was if he would get make-up presents for missed birthdays and Christmases. I said no; Art said absolutely, and for a solid two months, he brought Max a present every day.

Spoiled rotten doesn't begin to cover it, but I can't deny Artemis anything where Max is concerned. Not when it's my fault he lost so much time with him. Not when he's such an amazing father. His love for Max was instant, and their bond is unbreakable.

It pushed Artemis to do what he wanted to do all those years ago and had hoped to accomplish the night we got trapped at the airport...to break away from the Warren fold.

Telling the two senior Artemises that he was leaving Warren Enterprises was like a slap in the face to them. Artie never wanted to hurt them, despite all the ways they've hurt him over the years, but he made it clear there was no convincing him to stay.

His heart was with Max and me. And our hearts would always be at home in Cape Harmony. Even if it meant living without the Warren fortune at our disposal.

The way they cut him off stung, but it was the break he needed to truly move forward.

And we have. Our lives have completely changed since that day only six months ago at that Godforsaken airport.

Art's no longer a CEO apparent of a multibillion-dollar family business, and I'm no longer in the music biz. While it hurt to give up my dream, coming back to Cape Harmony is exactly what we all needed. A reboot where it all began.

A new law firm, where Art can take whatever cases he wants, including pro bono work he's always dreamed of. Me working at Mom and Dad's store. They always intended me to take over, and they were hurt when I said I wanted something else in life. Returning to them and the family business couldn't have thrilled them more.

And a beautiful house on the beach where I can watch my family frolicking in the sand is all I could ever hope for.

That day in that tiny airport, I thought my world had been turned upside down and my life was falling apart. But the reality was...everything was just falling into place.

I tip out the last of the shrimp boil onto the newspapers spread out on the picnic table on the porch.

Mom's voice carries out the screen door. "Hey, Archie!"

Their muffled conversation floats out to me, and a few moments later, a deep masculine drawl greets me. "Hey, Pen. How are you?"

I turn to Archimedes. It still surprises me how much the two look alike. More like twins rather than brothers separated by two years. "Archie, how are you?"

He closes the distance between us and pulls me into a one-armed hug, the other holding a bottle of wine. "I'm good, thanks. You look well. Where's that shitty brother of mine? He doesn't have time to call me anymore."

It's said jokingly, but examining his face, I can tell he's half-serious. For so long, Artie was always around, at everyone's beck and call, doing whatever anyone in the family needed. Those days are long gone, and while I know Archie is happy for his big brother, I think deep down, he really misses him and just isn't able to say it without trying to pass it off as a joke.

Plus, ever since Art left the Warren fold, all of his responsibility has fallen to Archie. And I'm sure that's a heavy burden to bear.

"Let me take that." I reach for the bottle of wine.

Knowing him, it's impeccably suited to pair with this meal. For the Warrens, nothing is better than good food and wine. No doubt, this bottle will go perfectly.

Some things even I can't fault the Warrens for.

I wave my free hand toward the beach. "Can't you tell by

173

the squealing? He's out there chasing Max around in the sand. Go on. You should take your shoes off and get out there and join them. A little walk and some fresh air might just do you some good, City Boy. Help you clear your head. I'll call when it's time to eat."

He leans back against the sun-bleached wood siding of the old house and crosses his arms over his chest. "I don't want to interrupt them. He looks really happy." He gazes out across the beach to his brother and his nephew, a huge smile plastered on his face. "Honestly, Penelope, I've never seen my brother happier than when he's with you and Max."

Archie puts on a harsh façade at times, but deep down, he's a gigantic softie.

And he's going to make me cry.

He just looks so lost. Even more so than the last time he came to visit us at Easter.

I reach out and grasp his forearm. "One day, you'll find someone, and she'll make you just as happy. Don't make the same mistakes we did, Archie. Don't waste time. Don't let her get away. If you find her, hang on to her with everything you've got."

Archie bites out a humorless laugh. "That isn't in the cards for me, Pen. I'm lucky if I get to leave the office with enough time to go home to eat, shower, and change before heading right back. Father didn't take Art's leaving very well. I'm paying for it. I'm virtually chained to the desk right now."

Shit.

Art worried this would happen. That their father would come down full force on his brother once he left.

"I'm sorry, Archie. We didn't intend to make things harder for you."

"You didn't, Penelope, really. Our father is a ball buster. And it's what I've always wanted, truth be told. I envied Artemis and what he got for being the eldest and named after

Father and Grandfather. I asked for it. It's just been a while since I've been under that kind of pressure. Art's been his punching bag for so long, I almost forgot how good I had it."

Little footsteps bound up the deck, and Max grabs Archie's hand before I can stop him.

He's probably covered in sand.

"Uncle Archie! Come help me build a sandcastle! Come on! Come on! Let's build a sandcastle!"

Archie squats down and ruffles Max's already wild and windswept hair. "Hey, Little Man! How's my favorite nephew?"

"I'm your only nephew, Uncle Archie!"

A grin spreads across Archie's lips. "You got me there, buddy. But it's still true. You're my favorite."

He kicks off his shoes and lets Max drag him out onto the sand, despite really not being dressed for it.

I chuckle and grab the silverware to set the table. The door swings open behind me, and Dad sets down a large bowl of salad.

His wise eyes rake over the scene on the beach—Archie and Artemis elbow-deep in the sand, trying to help Max build his vision. "I'm glad you're here, Pen. I think this Christmas is going to be one to remember."

His words have tears burning in my eyes. "You're right, Dad. It will be."

He grins at me before disappearing back into the house to help Mom. I glance back at the beach to find Artemis striding across the sand toward me.

I can't help but think of that young man who I gave my heart to on the same beach so many years ago. I'd do it all again if we ended up right where we are now.

Well, I might change a few things.

He comes up the steps and around the table to me. "You need any help, Pen?"

His arms slide around my waist from behind, drawing me back against him. His lips skim the column of my neck, leaving goose bumps in their wake.

I turn in his arms. "What kind of help are you offering, Mister Warren? I've got some ideas." I waggle my eyebrows suggestively and press my body against his.

He laughs, and those little lines I love so much bracket his smile. "Nothing I can say in front of mixed company, Miss Barnes."

"Daddy! Come help us build a castle!"

Max falls over in a fit of giggles as Archie struggles to get the sand to stick together into any sort of shape.

Archie looks up at the porch and waves at us. "Yeah, Dad! I suck at this. Get your ass out here!"

"Yeah, Dad, Uncle Archie sucks at this! Get your ass out here," Max repeats verbatim.

Artie narrows his eyes on Max and shakes a finger at him. "Maxwell Warren, you don't talk like that. That's not nice."

We both struggle to contain our laughs. Max heaves out a sigh and returns to assisting Archie with what is turning out to be a very pathetic looking sandcastle.

Artemis' arms tighten around me. "Now...about those ideas of yours." His lips meet mine. "Surprise me later?"

I kiss him back and melt just a little bit more, fall in love just a little bit more with Artemis Warren, if that's even possible. "You can count on it."

He squeezes me tightly before heading out to help Max and Archie.

Watching the two greatest loves of my life play in the sand is like a damn dream. One that's only going to get better after dinner when I spring my surprise on Artie.

❄

ARTEMIS

Archie reclines back in his chair on the back porch and glances over at me. "Are you happy?"

Fuck, yes.

Except I don't say that. I can't, not with Max right beside me on the porch swing.

I grin at Archie. "I've never been happier."

"I hadn't noticed. That perma-smile plastered on your face gives nothing away."

I can't help but smile even bigger. It's hard to keep it in, how fucking insanely, deliriously happy I am.

He may give me shit about it, but I couldn't care less. Even his jabs can't break my mood. Not with what I have planned.

Archie sighs and stares out at the waves lapping at the beach. "Was it worth it? All the shit Father and the rest of them gave you for leaving? I don't know how you took it."

They about lost their shit when they found out about Penelope and Max, and, of course, they went straight into Warren mode, talking custody and lawsuits, but they really went apeshit when I told them I was leaving Warren Enterprises.

The backlash almost broke me. What they said still stings, still has me lying awake at night at times. But I was determined, and I finally stood my ground against the Warrens.

I almost feel sorry for them at times.

All their hopes and dreams, gone just like that.

Their reaction may have been warranted given all the plans they had for me, yet I found an unlikely ally in Grandmother. When she stepped in and told Mother and Father to shut it because I was a grown man perfectly capable and well within my rights to make decisions about my own life, I almost had a heart attack.

She said I knew who I was and where I wanted to be and, "Wherever that is, he is still a Warren."

No one argues with Ruby Warren.

No one.

So, that was it.

I walked away from Warren Enterprises. From Father's Senate office. From all the clients and potential ones I had cultivated in New York, all the allies I had, and I settled on this beach in Cape Harmony with the only two people who matter.

Things with the Warren clan may never get to a place where they'll accept my decisions, but it's a work in progress.

I may not have their money or power anymore, but I have Pen and Max. And Jolynn and Larry. They treat me just like I'm theirs, without the pressure and expectations Father and Mother always put on me.

But now, that's all been passed onto Archie. And it weighs on him. I can see it in the black circles under his eyes that get larger and darker every time we get together.

I lean toward him. "My sanity alone was worth it, but now...I have this." I spread my arms out. "And I have them." I point to Max next to me and then Pen, where she stands near the table with her parents.

It's the best feeling in the world. I never thought I could be so happy. The only darkness in the sea of light my life has become is what my decision has done to Archimedes.

"What about you, Arch? How are things going now that you are the heir apparent?"

He laughs, but the humor doesn't reach his eyes. "It's a lot of work, but I like it. Father and Mother are trying to rope me in and keep me on a tight leash, but I'm not so easily wrangled."

I snort and shake my head. "Of that, I have no doubt. You

know, if the shit hits the fan, you can always come work with me."

"Momma, Daddy said a bad word." Max runs to Penelope, and Larry scoops him up and carries him into the house.

Archie barks out a laugh. "I hate to break it to you, Art, but your son is a snitch."

I laugh and grin at him. "He's just honest."

That's something I can never fault him for. It's an excellent quality to have. One the Warrens seem to lack. At least it's not genetic.

Baby bro tosses me a grin. "So, how *is* your firm doing?"

I sigh and lean back on the swing, setting it in motion. "Decent, considering the clientele in Cape Harmony isn't exactly what it was in New York."

Handling everyday issues for the residents of our town is a nice change of pace from the constant stress of Warren Enterprises and juggling Father's political career, too, but there are times I miss it. Though, I'll never admit that to Archie.

"You need anything else, Artie?" Penelope approaches and drapes her arm over my shoulder.

I take a deep breath, grab her hand, and I slide off the swing. "Pen, I need to tell you something."

This wasn't exactly how I had planned it. Candles on the beach at dusk with the waves lapping at our feet is more what I had in mind. But the waiting has been killing me. I can't go another minute.

I drop to one knee, right in front of the woman who is everything good in my world.

Her eyes widen, and she presses her hand over her mouth. "Artemis, what… what are you doing?"

I dig in my pocket, pull out the red heart-shaped origami box, and hold it up to her. "Giving you my heart."

Tears glisten in her gaze, and I press the sides to expose the ring inside.

"Penelope Barnes, you are the love of my life. I was nothing, no one until I met you. You are everything in my world that is good, beautiful, and true. You pushed me to be a better person, to break away from the things and people who were dragging me down and making me become someone I hated. You've given me everything, and now, I want to give you something, my last name. Penelope, will you please marry me?"

The second of silence and shock on her face almost make me nervous.

"Yes, yes, yes, yes!" she shouts and flings herself into my arms.

The force of her slamming into me almost knocks us both to the ground, but I manage to keep us upright.

"I love you, Pen. You couldn't make me any happier at this moment."

She kisses me softly, her hands cupping my face. "I bet I can. I'm pregnant."

Pregnant? Did she say pregnant?

"We're having a baby? Are you serious?"

She nods, and tears of happiness stream down her face.

I push up from my squatted position, lift her off the ground, and twirl her in my arms. Then, I kiss her, my heart so full, it almost hurts.

I'm going to be a daddy...again!

I set Pen back on her feet and stare at the woman who has held my heart from the very beginning.

This...this is how it should have been all those years ago.

Just a city boy who fell in love with the beautiful summer girl and lived happily ever after.

❄

We hope you enjoyed *Holiday Terminal.*

Want more from the Warren family?

You can now grab two, *Holiday Bridal Wave*, Archimedes'
story:
www.books2read.com/HolidayBridalWave

*Wanted: one bride for marriage to billionaire heir at New
Year's Eve wedding. Submit resume and photo to
INEEDAWIFE@wannamarryabillionaire.com*

ARCHIMEDES

All I want is to be CEO at Warren Enterprises Worldwide,
but the newly revised Warren Trust makes it clear...
I won't inherit the company or the family fortune unless I'm
hitched before the first of the year.
Too bad I don't have a girlfriend or fiancée.
What I do have is charm, dashing good looks, a prestigious
lineage, an email address, and a faithful assistant willing to
help me sort through all the applicants.
But the longer we spend weeding out the duds, the more I
appreciate the woman in front of me.
Too bad Blaire doesn't fit the requirements for a Warren
bride.
And one way or another, this New Year's Eve, I'll be kissing
my wife at the stroke of midnight.

BLAIRE

Helping my hot boss find a bride isn't really part of my job
description.
It's busy enough around the office during the holidays
without having to comb through applications from vapid
bimbos who only want the Warren money.

But Archie needs my help, and I'm hopeless to deny him when he flashes me that panty-melting grin and sings my praises.

He says I'm invaluable.

As an employee...or more?

Because with every moment we spend together planning his loveless New Year's Eve wedding, my heart inches closer to falling in love with him.

Holiday miracles are the things of fairy tales, but this New Year's Eve, one might be found in the place they least expect it.

www.books2read.com/HolidayBridalWave

ABOUT THE AUTHOR - GWYN MCNAMEE

Gwyn McNamee is an attorney, writer, wife, and mother (to one human baby and two fur babies). Originally from the Midwest, Gwyn relocated to her husband's home town of Las Vegas in 2015 and is enjoying her respite from the cold and snow. Gwyn has been writing down her crazy stories and ideas for years and finally decided to share them with the world. She loves to write stories with a bit of suspense and action mingled with romance and heat.

When she isn't either writing or voraciously devouring any books she can get her hands on, Gwyn is busy adding to her tattoo collection, golfing, and stirring up trouble with her perfect mix of sweetness and sarcasm (usually while wearing heels).

Gwyn loves to hear from her readers.
Here is where you can find her:
Facebook:
https://www.facebook.com/AuthorGwynMcNamee/
Twitter:
https://twitter.com/GwynMcNamee
Instagram:
https://www.instagram.com/gwynmcnamee
Bookbub:
https://www.bookbub.com/authors/gwyn-mcnamee
FB Reader Group:
https://www.facebook.com/groups/1667380963540655/

Website:
https://www.gwynmcnamee.com

OTHER WORKS BY GWYN MCNAMEE

The Inland Seas Series (Romantic Suspense)

Squall Line (Book One)

WAR

Out on the water, I'm in control.

I don't make mistakes.

But the fiery redhead destroyed my plans and

left me no choice.

I had to take her.

Now I'm fighting for my life while battling my growing attraction
for my hostage.

Grace may have started my downfall, but she could also be my
salvation.

GRACE

The moment he stepped foot on my ship, I knew he was trouble.

He took me, and now, my life is in his hands.

But things aren't what they seem, and Warwick isn't

who he appears.

The man who holds me hostage is slowly working his way into my
heart even as greater dangers loom on the horizon.

War and Grace.

Dark and light.

Love and hate.

This storm may destroy them both...

Rogue Wave (Book Two)

CUTTER

Complete the mission.

It's what I was trained to do—no matter what.

But when things go to shit right in front of me, my objective gets compromised by a set of fathomless amber eyes.

This isn't a woman's world.

Yet, Valentina refuses to see how dangerous the course she's plotted really is.

How dangerous I am.

VALENTINA

The man who saved my life is just as lethal as the one trying to take it.

Maybe even more.

While he may have rescued me, in the end,

Cutter is my enemy.

The one intent on destroying everything I've striven for.

But the scars of his past draw me closer even though I know I should move away.

Cutter and Valentina.

Anger and desire.

Fight and surrender.

This wave may drag them both under…

Safe Harbor (Book Three)

PREACHER

When it comes to firewalls, no one gets

through my defenses.

For the past five years, protecting this band of f-ed up brothers has been my mission.

But Everly pulls me from my cave and does the one thing no one else ever has...

She makes me believe there's a life outside the world

on my screens.

Too bad actions have consequences, ones that threaten everything and everyone around me.

Including the beautiful tattoo artist who has managed to etch herself onto my heart.

EVERLY

The emotional upheaval of the last six months would be enough to break anyone.

And I can already feel myself cracking.

A tall, sexy, tattooed bad boy is the last thing I need thrown into the mix.

All I want is to keep my head down and pour my pain

into my art.

But Preacher walks into my life and offers me safety in a world where I thought there was none.

Until our pasts finally catch up with us...

Preacher and Everly.

Fear and loss.

Hope and heartbreak.

This harbor may be their salvation.

AVAILABLE AT ALL RETAILERS:

books2read.com/SafeHarbor

Anchor Point (Book Four)

ELIJAH

Life outside the walls of my prison cell is far harder than the time I did inside.

There, I had my misery to keep me company.

Out here, I'm forced to face the reality of

everything I've lost.

Nothing can repair the gaping hole in my chest.

Yet, a broken woman wrapped in chains threatens to unravel the tangle of excuses I use to keep everyone

at arm's length.

But letting Evangeline into my world means exposing her to the real threat.

Me.

And all the terrible things that come along with that.

EVANGELINE

Taken.

Enslaved.

To be sold to the highest bidder.

The monsters who stole me away from my life

have no conscience.

I'm not so sure the man who rescues me is any different.

He's an ex-con and a pirate— not to be trusted.

But the dark veil of anguish that shrouds him can't hide the truth of who he is at his core.

Elijah isn't the enemy.

He may be broken and tormented...

And exactly what I need.

Elijah and Evangeline.

Agony and regret.

Faith and acceptance.

This anchor may pull them both down...

AVAILABLE AT ALL RETAILERS:

books2read.com/AnchorPoint

Dark Tide (Book Five)

RION

There is no black and white in this life.

The line between right and wrong blurs.

I'm constantly crossing it.

Saving a life is just as easy as taking one.

And I'm damn good at both.

Finding a woman who can survive in this world was never on the radar.

But Gabriella pulls me from the bottom of a bottle and touches me in a way no one else can.

Too bad secrets and lies have a way of catching up with everyone.

GABRIELLA

How did I end up here, slinging drinks at a dive bar in the middle of nowhere?

The choices that brought me to this were never even a glimmer of possibility only a few years ago.

How things can change so fast…

And now, my path puts me on a collision course

with Orion Gates.

His bigger-than-life size and personality should

be a warning.

The profession he's chosen should be the ultimate

final straw.

But instead, I find myself unable to resist his pull.

A decision that could lead to the end of all of us.

Rion and Gabriella.

Lust and lies.

Betrayal and ruin.

This tide may drown everyone…

AVAILABLE AT ALL RETAILERS:

books2read.com/DarkTide

The Hawke Family Series

Savage Collision **(The Hawke Family - Book One)**

He's everything she didn't know she wanted. She's everything he thought he could never have.

The last thing I expect when I walk into The Hawkeye Club is to fall head over heels in lust. It's supposed to be a rescue mission. I have to get my baby sister off the pole, into some clothes, and out of the grasp of the pussy peddler who somehow manipulated her into stripping. But the moment I see Savage Hawke and verbally spar with him, my ability to remain rational flies out the window and my libido takes center stage. I've never wanted a relationship—my time is better spent focusing on taking down the scum running this city —but what I want and what I need are apparently two different things.

Danika Eriksson storms into my office in her high heels and on her high horse. Her holier-than-thou attitude and accusations should offend me, but instead, I can't get her out of my head or my heart. Her incomparable drive, take-no prisoners attitude, and blatant honesty captivate me and hold me prisoner. I should steer clear, but my self-preservation instinct is apparently dead—which is exactly what our relationship will be once she knows everything. It's only a matter of time.

The truth doesn't always set you free. Sometimes, it just royally screws you.

AVAILABLE NOW AT ALL RETAILERS:

books2read.com/SavageCollision

Tortured Skye (The Hawke Family - Book Two)

She's always been off-limits. He's always just out of reach.

Falling in love with Gabe Anderson was as easy as breathing. Fighting my feelings for my brother's best friend was agonizingly hard. I never imagined giving in to my desire for him would cause such a destructive ripple effect. That kiss was my grasp at a lifeline— something, anything to hold me steady in my crumbling life. Now, I have to suffer with the fallout while trying to convince him it's all worth the consequences.

Guilt overwhelms me—over what I've done, the lives I've taken, and more than anything, over my feelings for Skye Hawke. Craving my best friend's little sister is insanely self-destructive. It never should have happened, but since the moment she kissed me, I haven't been able to get her out of my mind. If I take what I want, I risk losing everything. If I don't, I'll lose her and a piece of myself. The raging storm threatening to rain down on the city is nothing compared to the one that will come from my decision.

Love can be torture, but sometimes, love is the only thing that can save you.

Stone Sober (The Hawke Family - Book Three)

She's innocent and sweet. He's dark and depraved.

Stone Hawke is precisely the kind of man women are warned about — handsome, intelligent, arrogant, and intricately entangled with some dangerous people. I should stay away, but he manages to strip my soul bare with just a look and dominates my thoughts. Bad decisions are in my past. My life is (mostly) on track, even if it is no longer the one to medical school. I can't allow myself to cave to the fierce pull and ardent attraction I feel toward the youngest Hawke.

Nora Eriksson is off-limits, and not just because she's my brother's employee and sister-in-law. Despite the fact she's stripping at The Hawkeye Club, she has an innocent and pure heart. Normally, the only thing that appeals to me about innocence is the opportunity to taint it. But not when it comes to Nora. I can't expose her to the filth permeating my life. There are too many things I can't control, things completely out of my hands. She doesn't deserve any of it, but the power she holds over me is stronger than any addiction.

The hardest battles we fight are often with ourselves, but only through defeating our own demons can we find true peace.

Building Storm (The Hawke Family - Book Four)

She hasn't been living. He's looking for a way to forget it all.

My life went up in flames. All I'm left with is my daughter and ashes. The simple act of breathing is so excruciating, there are days I wish I could stop altogether. So I have no business being at the party, and I definitely shouldn't be in the arms of the handsome stranger. When his lips meet mine, he breathes life into me for the first time since the day the inferno disintegrated my world. But loving again isn't in the cards, and there are even greater dangers to face than trying to keep Landon McCabe out of my heart.

Running is my only option. I have to get away from Chicago and the betrayal that shattered my world. I need a new life-one without attachments. The vibrancy of New Orleans convinces me it's possible to start over. Yet in all the excitement of a new city, it's Storm Hawke's dark, sad beauty that draws me in. She isn't looking for love, and we both need a hot, sweaty release without feelings getting involved. But even the best laid plans fail, and life can leave you burned.

Love can build, and love can destroy. But in the end, love is what raises you from the ashes.

Tainted Saint (The Hawke Family - Book Five)

He's searching for absolution. She wants her happily ever after.

Solomon Clarke goes by Saint, though he's anything but. After lusting for him from afar, the masquerade party affords me the anonymity to pursue that attraction without worrying about the fall-out of hooking-up with the bouncer from the Hawkeye Club. From the second he lays his eyes and hands on me, I'm helpless to resist him. Even burying myself in a dangerous investigation can't erase the memory of our combustible connection and one night together. The only problem... he has no idea who I am.

Caroline Brooks thinks I don't see her watching me, the way her eyes rake over me with appreciation. But I've noticed, and the party is the perfect opportunity to unleash the desire I've kept reined in for so damn long. It also sets off a series of events no one sees coming. Events that leave those I love hurting because of my failures. While the guilt eats away at my soul, Caroline continues to weigh on my heart. That woman may be the death of me, but oh, what a way to go.

Life isn't always clean, and sometimes, it takes a saint to do the dirty work.

AVAILABLE AT ALL RETAILERS:

books2read.com/TaintedSaint

Steele Resolve (*The Hawke Family - Book Six*)

For one man, power is king. For the other, loyalty reigns.

Mob boss Luca "Steele" Abello isn't just dangerous—he's lethal. A master manipulator, liar, and user, no one should trust a word that comes out of his mouth. Yet, I can't get him out of my head. The time we spent together before I knew his true identity is seared into my brain. His touch. His voice. They haunt my every waking hour and occupy my dreams. So does my guilt. I'm literally sleeping with the enemy and betraying the only family I've ever had. When I come clean, it will be the end of me.

Byron Harris is a distraction I can't afford. I never should have let it go beyond that first night, but I couldn't stay away. Even when I learned who he was, when the *only* option was to end things, I kept going back, risking his life and mine to continue our indiscretion. The truth of what I am could get us both killed, but being with the man who's such an integral part of the Hawke family is even more terrifying. The only people I've ever cared about are on opposing sides, and I'm the rift that could end their friendship forever.

Love is a battlefield isn't just a saying. For some, it's a reality.

AVAILABLE AT ALL RETAILERS:

books2read.com/SteeleResolve

The Deadliest Sin Series (Dark Romance)

WRATH (Book One)

All I see is red.

Blood.

Pain.

Rage.

It consumes me.

The moment he took her, wrath invaded my soul.

I only have one purpose.

End him and take back what's mine.

Love isn't always clean, and wrath is the deadliest sin.

AVAILABLE AT ALL RETAILERS: books2read.com/DeadliestSin1

AFTER WRATH (Book Two)

They took something from me.

Something that can never be replaced.

They destroyed something.

Something that can never be repaired.

Only one thing can appease the burning rage in my soul.

Unleashing my wrath on those responsible.

The Dragon will rise.

Death will reign.

Because wrath is the deadliest sin.

AVAILABLE AT ALL RETAILERS: books2read.com/DeadliestSin2

SURVIVING WRATH (Book Three)

I fled into the night and didn't look back.

I grieved.

I loved.

Then he appears.

Dark.

Dangerous.

I never thought wrath would find me again.

But you can't run from it.

Not when wrath is the deadliest sin

AVAILABLE AT ALL RETAILERS: books2read.com/DeadliestSin3

The Slip Series (Romantic Comedy)

Dickslip (A Scandalous Slip Story #1)

One wardrobe malfunction. Two lives forever changed.

Playing in a star-studded charity basketball game should be fun, and it is, until I literally go balls out to show up my arch nemesis. When I dive for the basketball and my junk slips out of my gym shorts, I know my life and career are over. There's no way the network can keep my kids' show on the air after I've exposed myself to millions of people. I don't know how Andy, the new CEO, can go to bat for me with such passion. I also never anticipate how hot she looks in a pair of high heels.

Rafe's dickslip has made my new job even more stressful. It's hard enough being a woman in a man's world without dealing with sex organs being publicly displayed when someone is representing the company. But he's an asset to the network, not to mention hot as hell. I can barely keep my eyes off him or his crotch during our meetings. Defending him to the board puts my ass on the line as much as his, but it's worth it. So is risking my job to fulfill the fantasies I've had about him since he first set foot in my office.

Things may have started out bad, but… some accidents have happy endings.

AVAILABLE NOW AT ALL RETAILERS:

www.Books2read.com/Dickslip

Nipslip (A Scandalous Slip Story #2)

One nipple. A world of problems.

I own the runway. Until my nipple pops out of my dress during New York Fashion Week and it suddenly owns me. Being called a worthless gutter slut by a fuming designer is the least of my problems. My career is swirling around the toilet like the other models' lunches. Until smoking hot Tate Decker steps in with a crazy idea about how his magazine can maybe salvage my livelihood.

It's less than two feet in front of me. Perfect and perky and pink. And the woman it's attached to looks absolutely horrified. I need to help her, and not just because she's beautiful and has a perfect rack. Using my position in the industry to expose the volatile nature of our business puts my career in jeopardy in an attempt to save Riley's. I'm willing to risk that, but falling for her isn't part of the plan.

When love and tits are involved... Things can get slippery.

AVAILABLE NOW AT ALL RETAILERS:

www.Books2read.com/Nipslip

Beaver Blunder (A Scandalous Slip Story #3)

One brief mistake. A world of hurt.

No panties. No problem. At least until I slip on the wet floor and go heels over head in front of my colleagues and half the courthouse. Returning to consciousness can't be more awkward, until I find out who my sexy, argumentative, and bossy knight in shining armor really is. My career may not survive my beaver blunder, and my heart might not survive Owen Grant.

Madeline Ryan tumbles into my life on a wave of perfume and public embarrassment. She falls and exposes herself in front of me, and I find myself falling for her despite the fact she fights me every chance she gets. Being a woman in a good ol' boy profession demands a certain brashness, but it definitely has me thinking, maybe litigators shouldn't be lovers.

With stressful jobs and big attitudes, going commando has never been so freeing.

AVAILABLE NOW AT ALL RETAILERS:

www.Books2read.com/BeaverBlunder

ABOUT THE AUTHOR - CHRISTY ANDERSON

Writing with a whole lot of sarcasm and humor, mixed with a bit of Southern charm, Christy Anderson ain't no sweet tea kinda storyteller.

As an author of romance, Christy believes it doesn't always have to be hearts and flowers; sometimes, it is dark and twisted, but romance nonetheless. She mixes terror, revenge, and a sliver of love and hope into stories about family, friends, struggles, blurred lines, and happily-ever-afters.

Christy lives in the beautiful mountains of Eastern Tennessee with her husband and 152 cats (not really, but close), where she enjoys writing one twist at a time.

Web Page (under construction): https://www.
christyandersonauthor.com
Facebook: www.facebook.com/Christy-Anderson-Author
Facebook Reader Group: https://www.facebook.com/
groups/461018120762644
Goodreads: www.goodreads.com/christy_anderson
Instagram: Christy_Anderson_Author

OTHER WORKS BY CHRISTY ANDERSON

The Killing Hours

(Dark Romance/Romantic Suspense)

The Hunted (Book One)

My heart beats furiously in my chest trying to keep up with the pace
I have set.

I am running as fast as I can but it is pointless.

They will catch me.

I am only delaying the inevitable, postponing my

fate if you will.

I know what will happen when they catch me.

It's the same ending every time.

Still, I push my legs as fast as they will go, my body aches from the
exertion.

I can hear them behind me.

They are closing in.

This is part of a twisted game.

The goal, to catch their Prey.

Me.

I am the prize for the Hunter.

I am the Hunted.

AVAILABLE NOW: books2read.com/TheHuntedCA

❄

Book Club Novellas
(Romantic Comedy)

Glory Hole (Book One)

Typically, I'm not the kind of girl to spy on someone.

Really. I'm not.

So why, you ask, do I have my eye pressed to the wall of my living room,

spying on him through my own private glory hole?

Have you seen Beckett Jameson?

AVAILABLE NOW: books2read.com/GloryHole

Rim Job (Book Two)

You would think going to Las Vegas to celebrate your best friend's wedding would be a great time.

You'd be wrong.I'm the kind of girl who plays by the rules.

Las Vegas is the place where rules go to die.

I have a checklist for my life, an order in which the things on that list are supposed to happen.

So far, all has gone according to plan.

That is, until one fateful night when I meet him.

My list wasn't prepared for him.

Frankly, neither was I.

What happens in Vegas doesn't always stay there.

AVAILABLE NOW: books2read.com/RimJob

Made in USA - Kendallville, IN
1186568_9780998018058
10.27.2020 1014